Ghetto Theory Publishing
Presents

"The Ménage A' Trois"

"Where All Your Wildest Dreams Come True"

Written By: *Madam Princess*

Co-Arthur: *G. Prince*

Ghetto Theory Publishing

Copyright

2014

Disclaimer

This is a work of absolute fiction! The author has invented and created all of the characters, dialog, and incident, which is purely a product of the author's imagination.

Any resemblance to any actual person's life, or lifestyle; living or dead is purely coincidental, and is to be associated with only the author's imagination, or creative thoughts and expression.

Contents

Part I

Jordan

Life is what you make it, you're mind dictates you're being, if you say you can you can, and if say you can't you won't. We live within our own minds fantasy!

And if you're living in a fantasy world, how real is that fantasy? What role do others play in our own mind's fantasy? Life then becomes an illusion acting out an unspecified time frame and then ending, and then we move on!   *Madam Princess*

Jordan was born biracial, half/black - half/white. His father was black and his mother was white but, Jordan took after his mother side of the family with very light skin. He had curly brown hair, and his facial features were a broad nose, with full lips. He had hypnotic blue eyes that when he looked at you, it would carry you into another dimension. He lived with his father's parents on the Lower-East side of town, not much of a chance for a white-skinned colored boy with a ghetto-street heart to survive the hood.

Jordan was a bright and charismatic person, his only weakness was his own insecurities about himself. He had dreams, but would never take the first step to make them come true. He would never allow any one to get close to him; he always remained at a distance to any one that wanted to get close. In time he developed a unique mannerism about himself, cocky and rude, but charming with a sense of humor.

Jordan never worked but expected women to give him money when he needed it. His charisma and charm would always con woman out of what he wanted to hustle out of them. It didn't matter who she was, a girlfriend, his grandmother, an aunt. He didn't know how to survive on his own because he always had a women taking care of him.

* * * *

"The Things Inside Us That Are Hidden Away"

Jordan was witness to a police shot-out when he was coming home from school. The man that the police shot was a neighborhood friend that Jordan had visited with on many occasions. Gangster Charlie was his name, he was an O.G. raised in the hood, that wouldn't hurt a flea. But his past was another story.

Gangster Charlie ran with the best of them, Bad Boy Floyd, Crack head Melvin, and Double O, poor souls who will never see the light of day, except behind prison bars.

Gangster Charlie use to tell stories to Jordan about how they robbed three banks in one day and spent all the money in TJ, a town across the border into Mexico.

Gangster Charlie was a little touch in the head from all the cocaine that he snorted, and shot-up in his day. Some say down the line that, that shit fried his brain, and with all the pills and drugs he wasn't sure where he was at times. At night you would see Charlie walking down the street carrying an AK 47, and swearing to him self that if any one was looking for him, here he was, "come and get me," he would shout.

It was one of these times that the police found Charlie, drunk and caring his AK 47 walking down the middle of the street in broad daylight, when the police order Charlie to drop his weapon Charlie started shooting, wounding one police officer and killing another. More police were called in and the neighborhood was surrounded and Gangster Charlie was shot sixteen times in all direction before he fell to the ground dead. It was a miracle that no one else was shot.

When Jordan seen what happened, his inner sense of feelings for Charlie came out and he walked up with-out thinking to Charlie's dead mangled body and kneeled over him to close his eyes. Jordan blamed himself for not being able to stop his friend from getting killed.

* * * *

"Never Shake Hands with the Devil"

To empty his soul from the anger that he felt he began training at the local gym, day after day he trained hard not even stopping to eat, and at night he continue to workout. Punching and hitting the bag, over and over. On one occasion there was someone watching him. He was fascinated with Jordan's style and his rapidness in hitting the punching bag. His speed and rhythm was remarkable, constantly hitting it over and over again without missing, without letting up, the man that was watching offered Jordan a proposition.

"Well young man I've been watching you, I like what I see. My name is Jim Alistair, my friends call me Big Al.

Jordan thought to his self, "Big Al…the only thing big on him was his head, his hands were small and soft like a female when he shook hands, but his big goon looking bodyguard scared the mess out of a nigga, and if you looked at him to long you'd swear that you'd be having nightmares!

"So what do you want?" Jordan asked him in a sarcastic voice.

"I'll pay you $3g's, for one night," Big Al said.

"Doing what?" Jordan replied.

"Street-fighting!" Jordan was offered the opportunity to enter the street-fighting ring.

"What the fuck? Hell Naw!"

"Ok, 5g's! If you win I'll double it... How about it? Jordan found the offer a little hard to refuse!

"When?" Asked Jordan.

"Saturday Night."

"You're not shitting me are you?" Jordan thought that anyone who would pay someone $10g's to fight had to be full of shit.

"That's right $10g's cash! As soon as you win," Big Al said.

"Deal?" they shook hands!

"Do I sign a contract?" Jordan asked...

"No, what for? Too much paper work! Is it a deal?"

"Deal," Jordan said… Never knowing that he would have to fight a big muthafucka weighing twice as much as he did..!

The night of the fight Jordan found himself in a back warehouse and about a hundred spectators cheering, betting and screaming at the referee all at the same time.

The referee read the rules of the fight, just one, come out alive. What the fuck Jordan thought, what kind of fighting ring is this? Jordan really didn't have time to think before this 6 ft. 365 lbs. Jamaican fighter with missing front teeth, and baldhead came running toward Jordan with anger in his eyes. He was the top fighting contender and they gave him the name of Snap, Crackle, Pop... because he would snap, his opponent's neck, crack his spin when he jumped in the air and land on his chest, and when he win he would popped his eye balls out with his thumbs.

Snap, Crackle, Pop race toward Jordan taking four steps, and he was in arms reach of him. Jordan ducked and slid across the floor to the other corner, and tried to jump out of the ring, but the spectators only grabbed him and threw him back into the ring, Jordan's only defense was to bring this big muthafucka down to his size by socking him dead in his balls as he towered over him to reach down and grab him. But, he surprise Jordan and grabbed him by his leg and began spinning him around, then let go and Jordan went flying through the air into the crowd. Jordan stood up but fell back down cause his head was spinning, he tried standing up again and said, to himself, "it's time to get the fuck out of here." But, once again the spectators thru him back into the ring. Jordan felt like a chicken being tossed to a wild animal, he realized right then that he was fighting for his life and this big-muthafucka' had to go down. Jordan raced toward Snap, Crackle, Pop, and slid down feet sliding in first and with one leap straight into his balls, and down the mighty giant fell. Jordan jammed his fist into his face. Right left, right left, right left, just like he was hitting the punching bag, and Snap, Crackle, Pop was out cold. Blood gushed from his face, his nose was broken hanging from the side of his face, his lips was busted and looked like a piece of beef liver swollen and bloody, his eyes swelled-up like a baboons'- asshole, not a pretty sight! The crowd was screaming, kill him, finish him off!

But, Jordan's sense of compassion would not allow him to kill his opponent. Everyone in the arena booed Jordan and angrily threw bottles and cans and any trash they could find on the floor of the arena. When it was over Jordan had been hit with a bottle in back of his head from an angry spectator. Furious Jordan jump out into the crowd and grabbed the spectator by the throat and began chocking him until he passed-out, then it took five security guards to subdue Jordan and bring him down to his knees.

The crowd went wild with the smell of blood in the air. Violence filled the air as the crowd raised their voices in shouting profanity at the attendant.

"Let him go", they shouted "Muthafucken son of a bitch. Let him go!"

Before Jordan was able to realize what was going on the whole arena was in turmoil, bodies was fallen down left and right all around him. Jordan pulled himself up with a strong yank and throw the security guards off in every which direction.

Alistair who had hired Jordan run out to rescue him and rushed him back stage to his dressing room. Jordan was pissed off.

"What kind of muthafucken shit was that??? Jordan angrily shouted.

"It was just the crowd, they get like that some times, all hyped up with the smell of blood in their nostrils.

"You should have warned me…!"

"Hey, no big deal… the crowd liked you, they were on your side."

"Fuck you, just give me my money, NOW!"

"Ok, ok, just wait a minute… tell you what, double or nothing for next Saturday's fight."

"NO, pay me now!" Jordan shouted.

"Ok, ok! I'll pay you now the 10g's that I owe you, and you come back next Saturday and I'll pay you double if you win?"

"And what if I loose?" Jordan asked

"No problem, you just pay me double…!"

"Fuck that...!" Just give me my money now and I'll call it even, and think about next Saturday…"

Jordan knew what kind of snake Alistair was when he met him, his instinct told him not to trust him, because of his sneaky paranoid mannerism. Always rolling his eyes around when he spoke to you, looking over his shoulder, and grinning with a sneaky sound coming from his voice.

"This muthafucka boarder's on psycho, if you asked me," Jordan said to himself.

Jordan had no intention on returning back to the ring that next Saturday, but a few weeks had passed and with helping his grandparents out with having their utility turned back on, and buying them some new furniture and a refrigerator that was top of the line, and of course filling it up with food. After that, Jordan spent the rest of his money "that he felt came easy" on flossing and showing off in the hood.

So by the time three weeks had passed Jordan was broke, and there he was again working-out his inner frustration on the punching bag. Jordan was really good, perhaps if he had a trainer and focused his attention on learning the boxing game from the inside instead of taking it to the streets, in a few years he could really become a middle weight contender.

Jordan walked down the ally shortcut from the gym on his way home. His mind was swimming with thoughts on how to get his hands on some more money. Asking Cathrine, whom Jordan liked to call Cat, was out of the question.

Cat had those hazel green eyes that would frighten you when she put on her eye make-up. She would draw a thin black line that extended out to her lashes and would use green eye shadow to bring out the color. One time Jordan refused Cat's sexual behavior that she got so mad at him; and stare him dead in his eyes and began to hypnotize him with a sinister erotic look as if she was a predator stocking her prey! 'That scared the fuck out of Jordan!'

Cat was also the type of woman that gave a man anything he asked for, but would smother him with her begging to see him night and day. She'd wear a man out in three days to the point that his dick felt like it was ready to fall off. So asking Cat for any money would be like selling your soul to the devil and then trying to run out of hell with your ass on fire…! No not Cat that would be too dangerous Jordan thought.

"Paths that Cross Unexpectedly in the Night"

On arriving home Jordan sat on the front porch of his grandparent's house. It had been raining all day, but now the moon was out and he could see the stars in the sky. The air smelled clean and fresh, as if all the world's filth and garbage had been washed away and what was left was only peace!

"Hello," A voice echoed through the sound of silence, as Jordan sat meditating.

"Me and my husband just moved in next door. I hate to disturb you, but I was hoping that you can lend me a cup of sugar. Oh by the way my name is Charmaine, what's yours?

"Are you talking to me?" Jordan asked.

"Yes, how long have you been living here?" Charmaine asked.

"Forever!".. Jordan replied.

"It couldn't be that long, how old are you? 20…!

"22, who are you…again?" Jordan asked with a confused look on his face.

"My name is Charmaine, I'm your neighbor…Me and my husband just moved in"

Jordan couldn't believe his eyes, this beautiful woman, talking to him, just-moved in...! Did she say "husband?" That word threw Jordan's thoughts off balance. "I'm sorry Ms. Charmaine; I didn't know that the place next door was empty. Is your husband at home now?"

"No but I expect him home soon, I fixing him a surprise dinner and desert but I ran out of sugar, is it alright if I borrow a cup of sugar from you? I'd run to the store if I had time, but I expect him home any minute."

"Sure it's o'kay…! Hand me the cup, I'll get it for you." Jordan reached for the cup out of Charmaine hand and briefly brushed up against her fingers feeling her soft skin. Her nails were long and manicured, with dazzling sparkles on them. Jordan thought to himself, "High Maintenance!" and walked inside.

Jordan returned with the cup of sugar and handed it to Charmaine.

"Thank you!" What's your name?

"Everyone calls me Jordan!"

"Hi Jordan..!"

"Hi, what do you do for a living Charmaine?"

"I'm an exotic dancer..! I work at the Gentlemen's Lounge in Beverly Hills. My husband is in the military and he's home on leave, he's station here in El Toro, we've only been married a year, that's how we met. He saw me dance when he was first stationed here and the rest is history. Well, Jordan thanks again for the sugar, tell you what, here's a guest pass for you to come and see me dance, bring a friend, everything's on me. Just ask for Charmaine at the door, and you'll be treated well. See you later."

Charmaine walked back into her house. Jordan just sat back down on the porch and couldn't believe what just happened. He thought, "Why would a woman like that move next door to me...? She did say she had a husband, I'm sure he's a nice enough guy, but how in the world did he catch her? I guess I'll just have to meet him and ask him his secret!"

* * * *

"There's More Then What Meets the Eye"

The next day was Saturday and Jordan did his regularly work out at the gym one hour repetition on the ball, and another half hour hitting the bag, and one hour in the ring with a sparing partner that wasn't any competition. After all that Jordan was bored, so he decided to jug home and take a hot shower. Jordan lived about 6 blocks from the gym so it took him only 12 minutes to reach home. After a hot shower Jordan was feeling a little wound-up, as he looked at his self in the mirror, then he notice the guest pass that was stuck in the corner of the mirror that Charmaine had giving him to come see her dance. For Jordan this was a young man's dream. He might never get a chance like this again in his life, to watch half naked ladies dance exotically all up in his face as he sat back and enjoy it..! "Who knows I might get lucky tonight," Jordan thought to himself. Jordan knew he had to look good, so he put on his best turtle neck pull-over shirt that showed-off his buff physic, he wear his black slacks, gold chain that hung three inches from his neck, he decided to slip on his double breasted leather three quarter length coat, and his black leather shoes. He stared at his self in the mirror and said, "Watch out ladies here I come!" But all he needed now was a ride!

Most of the time he wouldn't have any problem asking his grandfather to let him borrow his car, but this time he wasn't so sure. Pop's as Jordan called him wasn't in a good mood, so that meant that Jordan would have to take a little heat from him before he'd say yes. What the hell Jordan thought, what's the worst that could happen he'd get more pissed-off and say no in a dozen four letter words.

"Pop's I need to borrow your car tonight, what-do you say?"

"What the fuck you little shit always asking for something! Go head, but you-better bring it home in one piece." Pop's shouted.

Jordan was out the door, and jumped into his grandfather's 1984 Cadillac Coupe De Ville his pride and joy and was headed down the highway.

Jordan arrived at the Gentlemen's Lounge in Beverly Hills an hour later. As he entered the lounge a tall buff dude greeted him at the door.

"Do you have a reservation Sir?"

"Yes, I do!" Jordan replied with a cocky grin on his face, then Jordan flashed his VIP guest pass.

"This way Sir, please follow me!"

Jordan followed him to a booth that had a sheer red satin curtain draping down from the ceiling, and the table was right up front, attached to the stage.

The hostess walked over to his table and asked, "What would you like to drink Sir, everything is on the house for you tonight."

Jordan couldn't believe his eyes; the hostess that was speaking to him was wearing a tight-fitting spandex dress that revealed every little sexy curve of her body. The only thing that the dress was covering up was her tattoo that was on her butt. But her nipples, stood out like grapes on a vine ready to be plucked, and her ass was firm and tight. Jordan thought to himself, "I wonder what gym she works-out at!"

Jordan was trying to look her in her eyes but that was pretty hard to do, with her body looking so luscious standing in front of him.

"Well, in that case Ms., bring me your best Bottle of Champagne, and two glasses.

"Are you expecting a guest Sir?"

"Perhaps, I was invited by Charmaine to come and see her dance."

"Oh, I'm sorry Sir, but Charmaine will not be dancing tonight. But, her replacement who's name is Crystal will be filling in."

"Well I'm sure I won't be disappointed." Jordan replied.

The hostess returned with a large bottle of Dom Pirignon and two glasses. She popped the bottle of Champagne and opened it for him and poured him a glass. As she was standing there the music began playing and the hostess pressed a button so that the sheer curtains would close slowly leaving only a dim reflected shadow of Jordan sitting at the table. This pick-a-boo, atmosphere allowed for discretion on the clientele's part, to masturbate if he had the urge to do so and it did occurred on a regular basic when the ladies would dance for them.

As the music started, out walked the most beautiful girl Jordan had ever seen. She was wearing a satin burgundy floor length robe, and with every sway of her hips the robe would open just enough to reveal the unexpected. Crystal, gently untied the bow that was holding the robe together, and with that she let it slide off her shoulder and drop to the floor, revealing a black see-through teddy and six inch Stiletto heels. As the beat of the music became louder and louder to each seductive movement that she made, you could hear pulsating breathing sounds coming from the audience. Crystal was a pro at causing the clientele to sweat with every move that she made, erotic moves and gestures causing each clientele to fantasize their wildness dreams.

Each elite customer had his own individual close curtain, so it wasn't surprising that they would bring three or four of their own ladies with them to enjoy what ever pleasure they desired.

After Crystal performance Jordan was drooling at the mouth, his heart was racing and so was the erection of his penis. He rang his buzzard to call for the hostess, when she arrived Jordan asked, "I'd like very much if Crystal would join me for a drink?"

"I'm sure she would, the price for her company is a thousand dollars for one hour's companionship."

Jordan couldn't help but look surprise when she said, "a thousand dollars," he knew he might have to pay something but, "a thousand dollars!"

"Should I let her know?" The hostess asked.

"Well, just wait for a moment; I might see another girl that I might like to enjoy her company instead." Jordan replied in his cocky voice.

"All the girls that you will see dance tonight are very beautiful but, Crystal is the Queen. So just let me know Sir."

* * * *

"We Become a Product of Our Own Environment"

Jordan wasn't a dangerous person but his livelihood put him in a dangerous environment. Jordan had ran into and old buddy that was friend's with his father. What was surprising was that Jordan didn't remember anything about his dad. His grandparents who raised him wouldn't talk about there son. They would just say that he was too good for this life. Jordan didn't understand what that meant until he met up with his father's friend, his name was Peter Sods, but everyone called him "Peta'man."

Peta'man thought that he was every woman's dream come true, the only thang was that most women couldn't stand to be around him. He drove an old school Buick, with tented windows, and a sun roof. One day Peta'man stopped by Jordan's grandparent's house after arriving in town. Peta'man was living in Jamaica for the past twenty years, because he wasn't allowed to enter back into the States. It seems that Peta'man was once a big time drug dealer in South Central, back in the 60's – until, the law enforcement agency started cracking down on drug dealers. That's how he got his name, his clientele would see him driving down the street and they would holler out, "Peta'man's here, Peta'man's here, and all the dope dealer's would rush out from all cracks and corners just like cock roaches at night and make their purchase. Jordan's mom got hooked on that shit, and that's what happened to her.

Jordan's mom was a beautiful tall, blond hair party girl. Her and her girlfriends would come down to the ghetto slumming looking for a quick high, that's how his parents met. His dad was studying law at USC, his goal was to study Civil Rights and become an attorney to get his parents out of the ghetto. Jordan mother's name was Elizabeth, she met Jordan dad at a party where everyone was at on campus. Jordan's dad Earl, fell in love with Elizabeth at first sight, and invited her out the next week. Elizabeth showed up, and Earl spent that night with her, Earl called her Bethany.

Bethany was a spoiled white girl, but Earl didn't care. When Bethany got pregnant Earl wanted to do the right thing and marry her, but her parents' would not allow it. They forced Bethany to put the baby up for adoption, but Earl's parents step-up and took the baby and raised him. Earl, never saw Elizabeth again, he got caught up in the drug scene and with his homeboy Peta'man they was pushing crack cocaine strong and heavy. Before you knew it they had so much cash on hand that niggas was looking to jack them for it.

Earl moved out of his parent's house to protect them from other drug dealers trying to kill him and take over his territory. He rented a stash house on the South Side of town, and he and Peta'man set up a bunch of crack houses all over the L.A. area and had their workers dealing crack on a steady bases. They were rolling in drugs, money and boo's. You would see them at all the high society clubs, along with the most beautiful women in town. On this one occasion they were at the Pussy Cat Club in West LA, in the VIP lounge when two swoll niggas' approached their bodyguard Jimbo.

Jimbo was an ex-Marine, who came back from the military shell shock, but for the most part if he took his meds he was fine. But, this night when approached by these niggas' from South Side Jimbo didn't hastate to release his combat training and with one quick move he broke both their necks in a blink of an eye. The club was emptied in less then a minute and Earl and Pet was exited out the rear before the police arrived.

Earl and Pet had to go into hiding and Jimbo drove them both down to San Diego and snuck them across the border into Mexico. The police had found their stash location on the South Side and did a raid on it shooting all Earl's and Peta'man's workers, and confiscating one hundred and fifty thousand dollars in crack cocaine and $300g's in cash. Earl decided that it would be good if he left the country and the only way he saw out was to enlisted in the Marine's where he was sent over to Vietnam.

In the military Earl immediately rose in rank because of his leadership skills and abilities for the most part as he put it because, "he just didn't give a damn about killing a muthafucka!"

As Lieutenant he felt that he could make up for the hurt that he caused his parents for letting them down when he got involved with drugs. He didn't know his young son Jordan that his parents was raising but he would write letters back home to say that when he return home he would step up as a father and raise his son, but that never happened. Earl was killed in an explosion on an orphanage, while trying to rescue the children that were trapped inside.

The Viet Cong had been raiding small towns and villages and murdering old men and women and rapping young girls while kidnapping young boys and forcing them into military service. Earls' platoon was order to evacuate the town and rescue any casualties. Earl sent in two men from his platoon to spy out the town and report back if any Viet Cong where hiding there.

"Lieutenant Roberts, we're ready to leave!"

"Listen, you two are my best look outs I have, I need you both to stay together and watch each others backs."

(The Viet Cong were known for snipers attacts.)

"If the Viet Cong reaches the village before us then were in trouble."

"Yes Sir."

"God be with you men!" Lieutenant Robert's words reflected his concern for his men.

Two hours later the two men from Earl's platoon arrived back.

"Sir, the village is clear their scared and hiding in their houses. There's a building in the center of town that is being used as an orphanage and about fifty children and one old woman who is caring for the children are hiding there."

"We must evacuate the village before the Viet Cong get here!"

"Yes Lieutenant."

"Private Walker, radio headquarters' and let them know that we're going in to rescue the women and children and bring them out, before the Viet Cong get to them first."

"Yes Lieutenant!"

"Everyone move out, I wanna be in and out in 20 minutes, I'll head for the orphanage and Johnson you come with me, the rest of the platoon check out each and every house and get them out on the double. Remember no one left behind."

Earl's platoon made it to the village in six minute flat. Earl took the lead and motion with his hand for everyone else to enter the houses and bring everyone out. As Earl and Private Johnson reached the orphanage in the center of town they were spotted immediately by the children who ran up to them and began smiling and shaking their hands because them knew that they were there to rescue them.

Earl put his finger to his lips for them to be quit, and as soon as he did one of the older girl's ran to tell the old woman that the American were here to rescue them.

Earl motioned to Private Johnson to follow her and bring the others out and to hurry. Earl began holding his arms opened and moving his hands in an inward motion together all the children around him. The kids thought that he was playing a game, so they all followed him, running and laughing behind him. Earl motion again with his finger to his lips and made a hush sound, for them to be quit.

Then he pointed up into the trees and put his finger to his lips again and said hush.... and the children understood.

Everyone arrived to the designated spot in record time, except for Private Johnson who hadn't arrived with the old woman yet.

"Private Walker, radio headquarters and let them know that we've clear the village of civilians and we're on the move out but, Private Johnson hasn't arrive yet, so I'm going back to find him."

"But Lieutenant, the Viet Cong are moving toward the village they'll be here soon!"

"Private, I gave you an order, DO IT! I'm going back! No one left behind, remember!"

Earl ran back to the village to the center of town where the orphanage was located, Earl's instinct told him that something was wrong, as he move slowly in with his rifle loaded and his bayonet attached. As he got closer he saw Private Johnson laying in his own blood, at the entrance of the building, he had been killed by a Viet Cong scoot who was sent in ahead of the others to spy out the village and spotted Private Johnson leading the old woman out, but before Private Johnson know it, he was attacked when he step out in front of her and the Viet Cong was waiting and thrush his knife into Private Johnson chest before he could let off a shot. The Viet Cong spy was holding the old woman and one of the girls at gun point until the others arrived.

Earl spotting the situation crept-up on him from behind and with his bayonet, thrush it into his back before he could let out a sound. The old women began crying profusely so that the young girl ran over to her and put her arms around her to quit her down, Earl motioned for them to hurry out. The young girl run out toward the direction that Earl pointed to, but the old women who was about ninety years old, couldn't run fast so Earl pick her up in his strong arms and ran with her. But not soon enough, because just as he grab her and started to run a Viet Cong who had arrived was hiding in the trees throw a hand grenade at Earl that exploded, blowing off Earl's upper torso and the old woman that he was carrying in his arms. Earl's remains were never recover but a coffin was shipped back home decorated with honors.

Peta'man had gone down to Jamaica and hid out until he was able to get a new name and a passport to enter back into the county.

Peta'man sat down with Jordan and told him the whole story! Jordan never knew because his grandparents never told him what happened. They were so hurt behind their son's death that they could never talk about him. So Jordan grew up with feelings of animosity and fighting was his only way to release his emotion.

As Peta'man talked Jordan eyes swelled up with tears, he couldn't hold back the pain that come rushing forth. Peta'man grabbed Jordan as he began to yell and scream and bet him self in the chest to release the hurt and pain that was trap in his heart.

Jordan's anger encompassed his very being, and at night his thoughts were only on revenge, to get even with life, and to make up for him being here. Why am I alive? My mother should have gotten rid of me before I was born! He struggled with himself to find the answer - why me? Why am I here? But there were no answers!

* * * *

"Beware Of the Poisonous Venom of a Snake!"

As time went on Jordan needed money so, he hooked-up with a loan shark name Van Eddie, but everyone called him Snake and he lived-up to his name being slippery as a slimy snake. Jordan's talent for street fighting made him a valuable assist to Snake's operation. But in time a low down dirty snake will turn on his master that feeds him when opportunity presents it self, and so it happened.

Jordan had just scored a big hit for Snake and Jordan's share was fifty percent of all recovery loans. But, fifty percent of a hundred thousand dollars was more then Snake wanted to part with. So, Snake set Jordan up to be jacked. He hired two goons to hide in the shadows for Jordan when he arrived with the recovery cash, Jordan for some reason sensed an uneasy feeling when he pulled up to Snake's mansion, on the upper side of Beverly Hills. Not only were the security gate left open but, the Doberman were no-where to be seen. Jordan started thinking back, and each time he'd arrive with the cash the dogs would rush toward his 280Z barking and jumping on top of his vehicle trying to attack him. But this time all was silent. Jordan mumbled to his self, "What the fuck is going on??" As he slowly exited his 280Z driver side door, he noticed a shadow hiding in the entrance way of the mansion. Then when he looked to his right, he quickly noticed a spark of light as if some thing had reflected off a metal object. With out making a sound, Jordan re-adjusted his movement and place his right leg back into his vehicle and slowly reached into his console between the seat of his car and place his hand on the cold steel of his 45 automatic. Just in that split second a big muthafucka ran up to the driver side of the vehicle and forcefully slimed the door on Jordan lift leg that was still outside the door of the vehicle. Jordan, sudden reaction to pain, instantly cause him to react as he turned his body to his left and his right hand on his 45 automatic shot through the glass window, the hollo point slog hit his unknown attacker dead in his chest. As glass shattered in that split instance Jordan cover his face ducking down toward his passengers side seat to prevent the shattered glass from hitting him in his face. In a panic Jordan's only thought was to "get the hell out of there," putting his car in reverse Jordan accelerated on the gas peddle and punched the vehicle into drive and headed for the electronic security gate. The gate began to close Jordan glance through his rear view mirror and saw all sorts of nigga's running toward him shooting, with the Doberman Pinscher leading the chase behind him. Jordon's 280Z crashed through the electronic gates sending his vehicle out of control spinning forward into a brick wall that surrounded the property.

When Jordan woke up he found himself in a jail hospital ward, charged with destruction of property, trust passing and attempted murder with a deadly weapon. Jordan's air bags exploded on impact resulting in injury to his body. He had three broken ribs, fracture nose, and a concussion. Jordan at first was unable to remember what happened, but then everything started coming back to him slowly, he remembered his vehicle where he had hide the money inside the spare tire underneath the back panel flap in the trunk of his car. $100g's no one knew but him, except Snake suspected that it must be in his car, because Jordan was bringing him his share. So, Snake had to get hold of Jordan's car that was being held in Police Impound until Jordan could be released.

During that time of the incident the neighbor's must've called the police because they were on the scene of the accident before Snake's goons had time to reach Jordan in his vehicle when it crashed into the brick wall.

Snake know that the only way he could get that money was to get the car. But, the police had the vehicle towed to the Police Impound, and only Jordan could retrieve his property. But, Jordan was looking at doing time, if the charges stuck.

Snake had a crooked attorney in his back pocket that he used to launder his money, his name was Sly Evens. Snake called attorney Evens to make a deal.

"Hello Sly how's every thang on the legal side?"

"You know how it goes, you win some, you loose same!"

"How would you like to win some?"

"What are you talking about, nothing illegal I hope!"

"Now would I do you like that? Now listen, I have some-what of a situation with one of my workers, you see he turn on me and took me for 100g's. But that's not the problem, I know where it's at but I need your help in getting it. You can have your normal fee of 15% percent."

"Wait a minute Snake, if I'm taking all the risk then I want more then 15 percent, I want double! 30% percent and nothing less!"

"You greedy son of a bitch, I'd have you killed before I let you try and swindle me like you do your clients."

"Yeah, well don't you forget I know all your little dirty laundry payrolls, and without me you're business would be down the drain. So don't try to threaten me Snake, do we have a deal?"

"You Sly weasel, I have no other choice, but I'll remember this!"

"Attorney Evens, why are you here in my court room, another one of your crooked friend needs a favor?"

"Judges Mitchell, I'd like to file a motion to have Jordan Roberts, release on bail."

"Mr. Roberts' bail is set at five thousand dollars, is there any thang else?"

"No your Honor, just that all his property be release to him as well."

"Granted."

Jordan was notified of his release but, because of his injuries his doctor refused to release him.

"Hi young man, I'm Doctor Jamison I have your release form here but I'm not approving it until you get better. You've sustained some serious injuries so I'm having you moved to a private room in the hospital Intensive Care Unit. You'll be with us for another few weeks. Is there any one you'd like for the nurse to call and let them know where you're at?"

"No doctor, there's no-one!"

"What happened Sly? Why wasn't Jordan release?"

"His doctor refused to release him. There was nothing I could do!"

"What about his property?"

"He's the only one that can sign out for it..! We'll, just have to wait, Snake!"

"I can't wait, that's 100g's just sitting around for some one else to steal, I WANT MY MONEY...!

* * * *

Jordan was recovering in the hospital for two weeks now, his strength was coming back to him and he remembered everything that had went down during the accident. "I need to get out of this place before Snake finds-out that I've left. If the doctor discharges me Snake will find out and be waiting. I need to get the hell out of here before then."

Jordan ribs were healing but were still sore, his eyes were no longer black from his broken nose, and he could stand and walk.

"Nurse I'm still having a lot of pain can you asked Doctor Jamison to prescribe a stronger pain pill?"

"I'll call Doctor Jamison now he's on duty tonight, I'm sure it will be ok to give you something a little stronger for bed time."

It was 8:30 p.m. that evening, the night nurse came in with Jordan's pain medicine that Dr. Jamison prescribed for him. "Here's your medicine Jordan, take it and get some sleep!"

"Thank you nurse, I will!"

Jordan had palmed the pain pill off in his hand and didn't take it. He needed the nurse to think that he was fast asleep when she came back to check on him. Jordan laid back down for about 15 minutes then got his clothes out of the closet and carried his shoes under his arms and walked very quickly pass the nurses stations while she was away attending to another patient. Once Jordan got out of the ward he slipped his shoes on and headed for the elevator, then outside he caught a cab.

"Where to Sir?"

"Police Impound."

"I'm here to get my belongings out of my vehicle."

"Name and ID," the night attendant said.

"Jordan Robert."

"To get your vehicle out it'll cost you $2,500 hundred dollars that includes towing and daily cost for storage!"

"I just need to get my personal belongings out and I'll come back in the morning to pay for the vehicle." Jordan said.

"Ok, I'll walk you back and you could get what you need. I have your keys here, they were in the car when they brought it in. It's pretty bent-up, I heard it went straight through a brick wall. It's a miracle that no one was killed. It's parked over there, I'll leave you alone. Just come back through the front office when you leave."

"I will Sir!"

Jordan pulled opened the door on the driver's side and popped opened the rear trunk from the inside lever of the vehicle, then he went to the back of the vehicle and pulled the flap cover off the spare tire. He pulled out the spare tire and with a crowbar popped the rubber away from the rim and felt for the money. It was all there! The police had searched the vehicle but didn't find the money because they were sniffing around for drugs and when they didn't find any they marked the vehicle clean to be released to it's owner.

Jordan had no intention of returning back to the front office. He thought to his self, "who knows that son of bitch might have phoned Snake and he and his goons would be waiting for me at the front gate when I walk out. I don't trust no muthafucka when it come to $100g's."

Jordan stuff the money in a gym bag that he had in the trunk of his car and placed it across his back and started climbing the bob-wire fence that surrounded the yard. Jordan jump to the bottom of the fence and ran down the road to a gas station that was across the high-way. Once Jordan got to the gas station he went into the restroom and washed his face and straighten-up his clothes and hair, and brought a cup of coffee and started making chit-chat with the casher over the counter, "hopefully, some one will come in and give me a ride," Jordan thought to himself. A truck driver that was passing through on his way up North volunteer to give Jordan a ride and he accepted, and when the truck driver was pulling out of the gas station Jordan saw Snake and his caravan of goons speeding toward the Police Impound. Jordan just shook his head with a grin on his face and said, "That dirty son of bitch..!" As the truck driver pulled off down the road.

* * * *

"Jordan Comes Home"

Jordan at this point was getting pretty sick and tired of whoopin' ass and getting his ass whooped. But the fight game was a pretty good way for Jordan to make fast money and get it legit. So Jordan returned to where it all started his home town.

Jordan never realized how much he'd missed the smell of pine trees in the air, or the color of a blue sky at day and clear stars at night. All these things didn't exist in the big city. Jordan's grandparents had died a few years back, but Jordan didn't come home for the funeral. He felt "why should I," there was nothing left to go back home to, so he didn't. But now it was different, he needed a place to be grounded and to get his life back together.

During the time he was away Jordan had gotten his self mix up with a couple of loan sharks that he owed big money to, and on top of that he had a drug problem, a thousand dollar a day gorilla on his back that he wasn't able to shake off.

Jordan arrived at the bus station and stepped off. As he walked down the street to his grandparents' house, he remembered the time when he was twelve years old and Frankie Alvarado chased him home with a bat because Jordan refused to give-up his lunch money. Jordan picked-up a rock and threw it at Frankie and hit him dead in his nose and it started bleeding.

"You son of bitch..!" Frankie yelled. "I'll get you."

But Frankie was too fat to run, so he picked up a bat and threw it at Jordan barely missing his head. From that day on Frankie never tried to take Jordan's lunch money again.

Jordan got to the front door and walked up the steps to his grandparents' house and turned the knob. The old house was just as they left it. The smell of old wood rotting away, and the cold dusty room, brought back so many memories.

Jordan walked down the hallway to his old bedroom, grandma had his bed made up and his shoes were tucked neatly under it. Jordan sat on the edge of his bed and started crying. The pain of his childhood could not be erased. His tears only confirmed what he refused to admit, that he never got over the hurt of loosing his mother and father. And now his grandparents were dead as well. Everyone that Jordan had in the world was gone.

Part II

"Victor"

*He robbed me of my soul and spirit the harsh reality
of life after 10 years.*

*What are you left with? An empty heart, anger,
sadness, and being all alone! Not, having no one to call if
you're life depended on it! Where is the rainbow after the
storm? If there is evil should there not be good! So where
is it...?*   *Madam Princess*

Let me start from the beginning of my story to
answer these questions?

Crystal was only 17 when she discovered life. It
was on her prom night. His name was Victor. He was tall
and handsome with a dimple in his chin when he smiled.
He didn't smile much only at Crystal when she'd walk pass
the foster home where he lived on her way home from
school.

Victor's parents where the talk of the town when Victor was just a little boy. He doesn't remember much about what happen that night when his mother found his father in bed with another women when she come home from working at the Pleasure Palace Casino were she worked as a cocktail waitress and some times when money was tight she would fill in as a call girl, at a hundred dollars an hour to business men visiting from out of town.

Victor mother's name was Isabella, but every one called her "Bella" meaning beautiful. And she was very beautiful men would say. Her hair was thick with long black curls hanging down to the middle of her back.

His mother was Arab and his father was black, they met when he was in the Air Force and had visited her country when he was on leave.

They fell in love at first sight. Victor's dad married his mom and bought her back with him to America.

But, Victor's dad James was never the same because of the nightmares that continued to haunt him in his dreams at night. James would never talk about what happened, he would just sit in his old recliner chair that sat in the corner of the living room, his mind would be in a daze, and his eyes fixed on the green leaf wall paper that Bella had used to fix up their little house to make it more calming. The walls were painted a light cool green and the leafy wall paper added a touch of forestry to the room. Their house wasn't any different from all the other houses in the neighborhood each one lined up side by side, old and tore up. The outside wood was old and gray, rotting away from rain and mildew, and if a swift wind decided to blow through that area, you'd swear the house would be blown-away with it. The porch would creek when you'd walk up the stairs, four of them to be exact, and the old front door screen never did any good except to let flies in during the day, and mosquitoes in at night. The screen door had a safety latch and most of the time some one would always forget to lock it. But Bella was so happy living there, and as she would call it "their cottage among the trees."

Not long afterwards young Victor was born. Victor was a handsome little boy, with big brown eyes and a wide smile with full curly jet black hair, and caramel skin.

Victor favored James a lot in that they both had that same big brown eyes that would pierce right through you, when they looked at you. And when Victor smiled he had that same dimple in his chin as his dad James did. "That's were Victor get his good looks from," people would say, from his dad.

All the hood bitches in the neighborhood would come tip-toeing around James after Bella would leave to go to work at the Casino. But on this night it was James' birthday, he'd had a few drinks in him and was feeling good when Ms Teri the neighborhood slot with her promiscuous-ass came creeping over to the house.

Bella knew something was going on and she wanted to believe James when he made love to her, and would say, "Baby you know that it's all in your mind, I would never cheat on you baby, cause I love you". And Bella would fall for that line each and every time.

But this night Bella had forgetting to mention to James that she might be home early because, she wanted to surprise him for his birthday. She had made arrangement to have a sitter come by and pick up young Victor while she and James went out to a club to celebrate his birthday.

Bell as James called her had got off from work at 10 o'clock that evening. She got in her old bucket and thought to her self, "one day James is gonna buy me that new car he keeps promising," but she knew deep down inside it really didn't matter as long as the thought was there.

Bell, decided to stop by the liquor barn to pick up a nice $50 dollar bottle of Dom Perignon Champaign then she got back into her car and jump on the interstate highway to make it home as fast as she could. She was so excided that she wasn't watching how fast she was going until a police car swooped up behind her with his signal lights on.

"Oh shit!" She said as she glared through her rear view mirror.

She slowly pulled over to the curb as the police officer pulled up behind her with his search lights beaming straight into her rear view window. The reflection from his search lights was so bright reflecting-off her mirror that it boomerang back into her eyes, it was so blinding that Bella turned the mirror downward adjusting it to veer back into the police officer's vehicle.

The police officer slowly walked up onto the driver side of Bella's car and said, "Do you realize you were speeding?"

"No sir, I was getting off from work early because I receive an emergency call from home saying that my son was sick. So, I was in a hurry to get there."

"Where do you work?" The officer asked.

"I'm a hostess at the Casino off the highway."

"A hostess," the police officer repeated!

"Can I see your driver license and automobile insurance?"

Bella, open the glove box and pulled out a white piece of paper that her auto insurance was printed on, then she reached into her purse that was sitting on the passenger side and open up her wallet and removed her driver's license and handed them both to the officer.

The police officer looked at her driver's license and then shined his flash light in Bella's face. Then he looked back at the picture on her license, and said, "This picture doesn't do you justice" he replied. "Tell you what, I'm gonna just let you go with a warning this time, but slow down. You're too beautiful to have that pretty face of yours scared-up!"

"Yes sir, I will…..thank you!"

Bella breathed a big sigh of relief as the officer handed back her driver license and automobile insurance. "Wow, that was close she thought to herself." Then she waited for the police officer to pull away first, before she drove off.

Bella, looked over at the clock on her dash-board, "damn I'm running late," she thought to herself.

Because of the delay it was going on 11 o'clock. Bella, was worried that James would be asleep when she got home and wouldn't wanna go to a club. "Well," she said to herself, "we could still have a glass of champagne and I could give him his birthday present, 'making wild passionate love to him all night.'" Bella giggled to herself as she thought of the way James enjoyed having his sex served to him.

Bell, pulled up in the driveway, and as she turned off the engine she could hear music coming from the house. "Good, Bell thought, he's still awake." As she walked up to the door she notice that the screen was unlocked, well she thought that isn't a surprise, since it was August and the tempter that day had reached 102 decrees in the shade. But the lock should have been on the screen. The door was opened and Bell could recognize the song that was playing, it was Marvin Gays, "Let's Get It On."

It was James favorite song, he would play it each and every time they were making love. "OH, he must miss me," she imagined to herself.

She started pulling off her clothes as she walked down the hall way toward the bedroom. First she removed her shoes and left them by the door, and then she pulled off her jacket, unbuttoned her blouse and dropped it on the floor, and lastly she unzipped her skirt from behind and let it drop off her hips. By the time she reached the end of the hallway where the music was coming from she was standing in the doorway with nothing on but her g-string panties, and lace bra holding the bottle of Dom Pirignon Champagne in her hand.

As she stood in the door way of their bedroom the light shinning into the window from the street lights outside made the two figures in the bed under the covers obvious as to what was going on.

At first, all Bella could think about was turning and running out of there. But she couldn't move, her feet were frozen in one spot. She tried to scream but her voice felt like a knot in her throat that swelled up and began to chock her.

She had to see for herself if it was really James. So she walked around to his side of the bed and pulled back the covers and with one swift yank, snitched it off the bed. With a frightful look, James big brown eyes gazed back at Bella, the tears in her eyes stared back at him with a cold distant glare. And without saying a word she raised the bottle of Dom Pirignon in her hand and said "Happy

Birthday," and swung it with a hard swift hit onto his head. Blood splatter ever-which-way, on the pillows, sheets, walls and on her, as the sound of his skull cracked. Bella, looked up at the figure that was in the bed with James and couldn't believe her eyes, it wasn't Ms Teri, it was Ms Teri's daughter little Lisa-Lin, who was only 14 year old. Ms Teri would pimped her out to any one in the neighborhood that would pay $100 bucks for her young pussy.

Bella stood there with the bloody bottle of Champagne still in her hand, and walked around to the other side of the bed were little Lisa-Lin was lying and stared at her immature body that wasn't even developed yet. Bella asked, "Where's you're momma at?"

"She's at home drunk!"

"Get dress!"

Bella, grab little Lisa Lin by the hair and walked her down the hallway toward the door, as Lisa-Lin reached down trying quickly to grab the clothes that was on the floor in the hallway to cover-up her naked body. Bell, flung the screen door opened as she shoved Lisa-Lin out first and then she walked out, down the street to Ms Teri's house.

Bell, upon arrive at Ms Teri's door, kicked it in with one hard kick, it swung opened and Bell pushed Lisa-Lin in with a hard push as she fell to the floor crying.

"You charge my husband money for this little piece of shit? He was my husband, now he's dead because of you!" With that Bell flung the blooded bottle of Champagne at Ms Teri hitting her smack dead in the head, the force from the bottle cracked open her skull splattering blood and pieces of her skull every where. Ms Teri had tried raising her hand to block the bottle coming toward her head but her reflexes were too slow. She fell backwards in her kitchen chair hitting the wall and as the chair flow backwards her neck snapped, CRACK!

The sound echoed through the house as Lisa-Lin screamed. "You killed my mother!"

"You're welcome!"...Bell said.

Bell, walked out of the door and back to her house down the hallway, into the bedroom where James bloody body lied. Tears filled Bella eyes as she realized what she had done. She leaned over James lifeless body shaking him repeating over and over, "wake up, wake up baby, it's your birthday, I have a present for you!" James bloody lifeless body laid curled up in a fetal position unmovable. Little did Bella know that when she swing at him and smashed his skull in with the champagne bottle he didn't die right away, the shock to the brain sent his body into convulsion, causing him to cramp up, like a hard punch to the gut.

Bell, walked into the bathroom and got a wash towel, wet it and walked back into the bedroom and sat on the edge of the bed next to James bloody body and began wiping off the blood from his face. But the more she wiped the more the towel became bloodier, until she was just wiping blood onto his face instead of wiping it off. Bella's heart became numb as she slowly walked back into the bathroom and opened the medicine cabinet and reached for the bottle of sleeping pills that was in there. She walked back into the bedroom and removed her g-string panties, and her lace bra and curled her naked body into his side, then she opened the bottle of sleeping pills poured them all into her mouth and swallowed them. As the clock on the night stand tic away Bella kissed James on the lips and whispered "Happy Birthday baby," and then she feel into a deep sleep.

By the time the police arrived it was too late, Bell pause had stopped. The police officer who had arrived on the scene recognized Bell as the woman that he had stopped for speeding. He shook his head in disbelief and said, "What a waste!"

To this day Victor doesn't remember how his mother looked; he was turned over to Children Services and was passed from foster home to foster home, until a family permanently cared for him. His mother parents didn't want to have anything to do with him because he was black and they said, "That black nigga James stole our daughter from us and took her to America to die!"

Victor was always confused about what people thought about him so he did his best to prove everyone wrong. But Victor was scarred by the death of his parents.

His faster parents would say to him, "you're just like you father a no-good-son of a bitch." And Victor heard it so much from them that after a while he believed it, and give up trying to do anything good.

* * * *

"Victor A Man on a Journey"

Victor had a hard time forgetting his childhood. Nothing was there except the memories of his parents. So Victor went off to the Marines to prove something to his self and all who knew him. In the Marines he became a spy informant, specializing in secret intelligence.

His ability to locate the enemy and infiltrate their headquarters and send back information on their whereabouts and have them destroyed, was a special gift. He blended into the population because of his skin color and looks; he became virtually invisible to the enemy.

He was a master sharp shooter and an export in hand to hand combat. You would never imagine it because of his physic. But he could bring down a six feet, four inch, three hundred pound assailant with his bare hands and kill him instantly in one swift blow of his hand.

Victor was assigned to a secret mission and on assignment an incident occurred where his cover was blown. His counter-part Izzy Taylor grow-up in the Bronx and had a taste for beautiful women. Taylor thought of himself as a ladies man, and all the women that he met couldn't resist his pretty boy looks and sexy charm. Taylor's bad habit for beautiful women always got him in trouble, and so it happened when on assignment. Taylor was involved with a beautiful woman intimately, but he was unaware that she was a spy for her country searching out co-opt agents. Elena never let on that she was being paid a large sum of money to reveal the identity of undercover agents. But, Elena knew that her lover was a spy but her orders were to bring in "Big Dog" which was Victor's code name.

The Bureau knew that somewhere information on their weapons location was being leaked out. Secret Intelligence would find a hiding place to store arsenal in enemy territory and one by one they were being blown up and American solders guarding the location were killed.

"This has to stop!"

"Yes General...!"

"It's vital that no one knows about this secret mission except you and me. I believe Captain that there's a double agent leaking out information as to the whereabouts of our weapons across enemy lines. We need our best man on this."

"General we do have several undercover agents working in enemy territory. One in particular who's code name is "Big Dog!"

"Can we trust him?"

"Yes General."

"Ok, get a massage to him and have him call me on my private line."

"Yes General, right away!"

Victor accepted the assignment, "how hard can it be?" He thought to himself, "tell no one about this, not even Taylor, search out the double agent and kill him! Easy..!"

Taylor's involvement with Elena was kept a secret from Victor. But, Victor wasn't that stupid not to see that Taylor had a woman on the side. Victor received a coded message saying that the weapons location was being hidden in an abandon warehouse underground, a hundred miles from the center of town and was being guarded by American soldiers patrolling the area.

Victor knew he had to get to that site and investigate any suspicious activity. He also knew that the area would be off limits to civilians so he had to come up with a disguise. Victor snuck onto an American military base that was station there and stole an officer's uniform and a jeep and drove out of the city. Two hours later as he approached the designated area he was suspicious and stopped the jeep and headed on foot toward the warehouse. As he approached he noticed enemy civilians loading military weapons onto three civilian trucks, and there were no American soldiers in sight. Victor got close and ran around the back of the warehouse to take a look at who was giving the orders. It didn't take long for him to see that the double agent was Taylor.

Taylor had orchestrated the whole plan and standing next to him was a beautiful woman with long dark hair and a fine sexy body that any man would go crazy over, most differently Taylor. Taylor's whole game plan in blowing up the locations where the weapon were being stored was only a cover-up for stealing the weapons and selling them on the black market, murdering the soldiers was necessary so there wouldn't be any witnesses. Victor had to do something before they got away with it again.

Victor ran back to where he had left the jeep and grabbed the AK 47 submachine gun and a box of hand grenades, from the back of the jeep.

"What the fuck I'm I doing? One thing for sure it's either do or die!" Victor's mind was racing inside his head he only had a short time before all the trucks would be loaded and he had only one chance to stop them, before the weapons landed on the black market.

Victor put the jeep in drive and punch it, the jeep race straight toward the trucks in high speed and with three feet in front of them he jump out rolling on his back armed with the submachine gun and hand grenades. The jeep went crashing into the trucks loaded with American admonition and exploded one by one as the trucks fire blast ignited each one. Victor broke and ran from the explosion firing shots wildly shooting the enemy men that had ran from the blast. The other men not hit began returning fire hitting Victor in his right shoulder and grazing his neck as bullets flew by.

Taylor and Elena stood there watching as the trucks exploded. Victor ran for cover behind a water tower that was used for emergency water supply.

"What the fuck is going on? And who the hell is that?" Taylor screamed..!

Elena, who was running for cover as the shooting began, let out a yell, "BIG DOG...! You fool."

"It can't be...!" Taylor yelled back, confused.

Victor threw two hand grenades up into the water tower platform and ran to a vehicle that was park around the side of the warehouse. Elena and Taylor continued shooting at him as he started the vehicle up, and began shooting back in every direction. Suddenly the water tower exploded and gallons of rushing water came barrowing toward them flooding everything in sight. Smoke from the explosion filed the air. American helicopter started flying over the designated area. Elena and Taylor manage to escape in and American military vehicle and drove away. The helicopters circling didn't suspect the vehicle as it drove off.

The Black market racketeers who had paid Taylor to deliver the weapons to them weren't happy to find out that their money and weapons were gone. They swear to kill the one responsible for their lost, namely "Big Dog." When the plot against Victor's life was revealed he was smuggled out of the country and his counter-part Taylor was found shot six times in the head, lying in his lover's bed and Elena was found naked in the shower with her throat cut.

When Victor returned back to the states because his identity was no longer a secret, he was assigned a training position for new recruits, but he was no longer interested in the Military so he resigned.

Part III

Crystal

"Where Is the Shadow of My Enemy That Has Turned Their Hand Against Me?"

Crystal would see Victor looking at her as she walked home from school and she tried not to make eye contact. But, the harder she tried the more difficult it became. One day she was trying so hard not to look at him that she walked right into a tree, because she wasn't looking where she was going. She bumped her head so hard that a knot swelled up on her forehead the size of a quarter. Victor started busting up laughing, that Crystal started crying from embarrassment, and ran all the way home. After that Crystal would take the long way home from school to avoid walking pass Victor's house.

Crystal as a young girl was never very popular, but she did have something about herself that no other girl had, and that was the talent to get what she wanted. She lived on the poorer side of town where dreams was all a young girl could afford to have. But, she thought to herself with the right looks and a fine body she'd be able to walk right out of that town and no-one could stop her.

Crystal was extremely smart, she spoke three languages, France, Spanish, and of course English. She graduated high school with honors, and was voted "Most likely to succeed."

With that background, Crystal attended one of the most reputable Universities in California, and with her looks and her talent she was invited to join all the elite sororities. But, Crystal focus hard on her classes, she wasn't there to blow a hundred thousand dollars worth of education on just partying. But, little did Crystal know that *"some times life throws you a curve that you're not ready for!"*

It was her senior year in collage and Erika, Crystal's roommate persuaded Crystal to go with her to a party that was on campus.

"Come on Crystal, come with me! I promise you won't regret it. Anyway it's your birthday, you're not going to stay in and just study, are you?"

Erika was known on campus as being the biggest hoe out there! And her nick name with all the football players was, "Hoe-ology," because as they put it "she came to collage to major in being a 'hoe.'"

Crystal's roommate Erika, knew of this party that the Alfa-Alfa-Y, was giving and everyone was invited. Alfa-Alfa-Y was one of the most elite sororities on campus, so without thinking and in need of some serious R&R Crystal decided to go.

"Crystal girl, you're not wearing that to the party are you?"

"What do you mean? What's wrong with what I'm wearing?"

"Nothing girl, except you look like you're going to a funeral, instead of a party. Girl, let it hang out..! No ones going to say anything."

Erika was so revealing with her clothes, you could see right through the out-fit that she was wearing, and wondering why in the world would she even try putting on any clothes at all, if all it did was show off everything anyway? Crystal's mind was taking her into a whole nother-level that she didn't wanna go there.

"O'kay, Erika you're right, I'll go change! Do you have something that I can wear?"

"Sure girl, try this on!

"Erika, what the hell is this, a bandana?"

"No girl, it's a dress!"

"A dress, and how am I suppose to put this on?"

"It stretches..!"

"Into what?"

"Just put it on Crystal and let's go. We're going to be late and all the fine men will be hooked-up with all the hoochies."

Crystal began loosing up once she got to the party; she began drinking and dancing with one of the most popular boy on campus. His name was William Van-Eddy, but everyone called him Willie. He was on the football team and all the girls' drooled over him. But, Crystal was the one that Willie had eyes for at the party. Inside the party it was so hot and smoky; all the students were dancing, drinking and getting high. Liquor was flowing in every direction, and there were kegs of beer lined-up ready to be opened. Crystal was attracted to Willie and was wondering about the possibilities as to where this would go?

"Crystal you're very beautiful, would you like to dance again," Willie asked?

The song that was playing was, "The roof, the roof, the roof is on fire." Not a favorite song of Crystal's..!

"It's pretty hot in here, maybe I'll have something cold to drink, and wait for the next song to come on."

"Ok, I'll go get you something cold to drink." Willie offered.

Crystal as naive as she was, she wasn't aware of what went on at these frat parties, she had just met Willie and convinced herself that he was a nice person, "after all he is on the football team," she argued with herself.

"Here Crystal, here's your drink, I made it especially for you!"

"Thank you Willie and Crystal kissed him softly on the lips.

"This is my favorite song, 'Loving You, by Minnie Ripperton was playing,' go ahead, down that drink so we can slow dance off this!" Willie said as he shoved the drink into Crystal face forcing her to take large gulps to finish it off.

Crystal didn't know that her drink had been laced with Ecstasy, before she was aware of it she began feeling dizzy, her head was spinning around and she couldn't stand up straight or even walk.

"Are you ok, Crystal?" Willie asked.

"No I'm not feeling well!"

"Ok, don't worry, let's go outside and get some fresh air, I'm right here with you, I won't leave you alone."

But all Crystal saw was a bunch of guys standing out back in the parking lot next to her car, and before she knew it she had passed-out.

When she woke up she found herself in a dirty motel room naked, where she had been rapped several times and had bruises and scratches up and down her legs, arms and wrist, where she had been tide and held down. She staggered out the door and looked around, her car was parked in front of the Motel room but she didn't remember anything. She staggered as she walked to the office and stumbled into the doorway. "Please help me, I've been rapped!" The desk clerk immediately dialed 911.

The paramedic arrived on the scene with two police officers' one male and the other female and she was taking to the hospital.

"Hi Ms., my name is Officer Mc Clain, I'll be taking your statement about what happened to you last night." The female police officer said.

"I don't remember anything, except waking-up in that Motel room."

"Do you remember what happened prior to that?" Officer Mc Clain asked.

"I was at the Alfa-Alfa-Y party on campus. I was dancing with Willie and it was hot inside so he offered to get me a cold drink. The music started playing again, and Willie wanted to dance off the song that was playing and he said, "hurry-up and down your drink fast, before the song goes off." So I did, but then I started feeling dizzy and Willie walked me outside for some fresh-air, but all I saw was these guys standing by my car, then the next thing I know I was waking up in a motel room that I don't remember how I got there, and my arms and legs were bruised and I had no clothes on.

"You said that you where dancing with Willie?"

"Yes, Willie Van-Eddy, he's on the football team!"

"We received a statement from a William Van-Eddy that states he was with a girl and they got into an argument and she stormed off in her car and left the party. Would that be you?"

"No, that's not true, we didn't have an argument?"

"Are you sure? You said that you can't remember anything?"

"No, I was having a good time dancing with him. We didn't argue!"

"You know Ms., the Van-Eddy's are well known in the community, and their son is on the honor roll, and volunteers at the hospital. His ambition is to be a Pediatric Surgeon. I think that you need to try to remember what exactly happen before you start bringing about accusation against someone.

Crystal realized she was screwed, and the police wouldn't do a damn thing about the rap.

They kept Crystal in the hospital for two days to run test and to check for HIV, and other transmitted deceases. Then she was released and went back to her dorm.

Erika's two friends Pam and Jackie who was aware of what Erika had done, because of her bragging about setting Crystal up, stop by her dorm room.

"Girl if that was me you would've set me up too and let those stinks from the football team rap me." Pam said.

"Naw girl, Willie and his friends wouldn't want your skinning ass."

"Yeah but you know girl that you was wrong Erika." Jackie said.

"She wasn't none of my friend any way. She thought she was all that, she's no better then me, that's why I did it, to teach her a listen!"

"Erika you full of shit, you better hope she doesn't find out, cause your ass is toast. Pam said, keeping it real with her.

"She ain't gonna do shit..!" And you two better not tell either, or I'll have Willie fuck over you too."

As Crystal entered her dorm everyone was staring at her as if she had just walked in naked. She went straight to her room, and setting on her bed gossiping on the phone was her room mate, Erika.

"What the hell did you let them do that to me?"

"What? I didn't know anything was going to happen? Willie just paid me to bring you to the dance!"

"Paid you..! How much?"

" Hundred dollars.!"

"A hundred dollars, that's all? Bitch, you sold me off for one hundred lousy dollars? What? Now you starting a new career Erika, pimping girls on campus? Bitch I should kill you! I thought you were my friend... then you gave me that hoochie dress of yours to wear to that damn party. You was setting me up! What if I'm pregnant, or got HIV, then what Erika?

"I was going to do it myself, but Willie said, he wanted a virgin!"

"Bitch you lying! I know I'ma kill you now..!"

With that Crystal grabbed Erika by her hair and snatched her off her bed. Then Crystal grabbed the computer that was sitting on the desk and pick it up and slammed it to the ground right on top of Erika's chest. Erika screamed for help and everyone come running down the hallway. Pam and Jackie jumped on Crystal's back trying to pull her off Erika, and when Crystal still didn't let go Jackie pick up a lamp that was sitting on the desk and smashed it across Crystal head. Blood gushed out from the cut and poured down her face as she fell to the floor. Jackie and Pam grabbed Erika and started out the door. Crystal rose up off balance and reached for a chair that was at the desk and throw it toward the door hitting all three across the back. As each one fell to the floor Crystal ran over to them with a broken chair leg in her hand and began betting each one in the face with it, hitting them over and over again as they screamed for her to stop. Crystal pulled Erika up off the floor by her hair and with one hard push flung her out the door. Then she grabbed the other two girls by the legs and pulled them into the hallway. Crystal stood there with blood running down her face and hollered, "What the fuck are you looking at..?" Screaming at the crowd that was standing in her door-way staring, then she slammed the door in their face so hard that the hinges fall off.

Crystal was mad as hell, she started throwing Erika's clothes, shoes, perfume, makeup all out the window two stories down. The campus police was called and Crystal spent the night in jail. The next day she was release and expelled from school. Her last semester and she was thrown out of school. Nothing happened to Willie and his gang-rap friends. His parents' paid a undisclosed some of money to the University to sweep it under the carpet and any DNA that was found that night on Crystal body was lost so the Prosecutor could not press charges. With shame and no money coming in Crystal swear she'd never let any one fuck-over her again, no one!

On her promise to herself, never to be fucked-over again Crystal started stripping at one of the most exclusive Gentlemen's Club in Beverly Hills.

Part IV

"Crystal connect with Victor and Jordan"

Crystal had a love for fast money, this was the one thing that all three had in common.

The only similarity that Jordan and Victor had in common was that they both had to prove something to the world, and most of all to themselves.

Crystal was the connection that brought them two together. She was still stripping at the classiest Gentlemen Club in Beverly Hills. She was now the highest paying stripper there. Victor walked in unaware that Crystal danced there. Jordan was sitting at the bar when Victor sat down next him. They started talking and Victor brought Jordan a drink. Then out walks Crystal in a mid night blue, baby doll lace out-fit and wearing black stiletto heels. Her jet black hair with the spot light shimmering off her body added even more mystery to her dark brown eyes. Victor at once was hypnotize by her almond colored skin twisting around the pole as she peeled off each layer of lace, piece by piece, that covered her beautiful almond colored skin.

Jordan was there every night, he was hired by the owner of the club to protect the ladies from the crazy drunks that got out of hand. But, to tell the truth Jordan himself couldn't resist Crystal beauty. And to make it worst he'd fly into a jealous rage if anyone else lusted for her. Damn that bitch is bad, Victor uttered. Jordan could never control his quick temper and before you know it, Jordan swing a quick jab to Victor's jaw, nearly breaking it to which quickly brought him out from under Crystal hypnotizing beauty.

"Man what the fuck is wrong with you." Victor said as he swung back at Jordan, and they both locked on and fall down between the chairs on the floor fighting, like two little boys on the playground.

"Why did you hit me?" Yelled Victor

"Man, I saw how you were staring at the ladies!"

"What man, the ladies are up there to stare at..!"

"No, you were doing more then staring, I saw you! You were lusting after her and using disrespectful comments."

"What the hell are you talking about, and who the fuck are you anyway?"

"I work here, I'm the clubs bouncer!"

"Work here or not, I'm sure they don't pay you to run their customers away."

Jordan turned around and looked and everyone in the club was gone...Out the front door in less then two minutes flat.

"Did you see that, I can't believe it..! These people must've never seen a fight." Jordan bitched.

"You call that a fight? Victor replied... "My grandfather hit me harder then you and he was sixty years old when he did."

"Boys, boys! Since you two want to run all of our money out the door, then it's only right that you both should go watch over my ladies at this bachelor party. And I expect you both to be on your best behavior or I'll personally punish you both. Crystal stood there butt naked in her high hills with two of her stripper on each side of her and they all had guns in their hands. Victor looked over at Jordan and they smiled and shook hands.

Part V

The Ménage A' Trois

Crystal and Jordan along with Victors became well known in owning their own club. They added gambling, beautiful women, and anything you could fantasies about. They catered only to the upper class clientele, the elite crowd. Mayors, Judges, Attorneys, Doctor's and the spoiled rich and famous, everyone who was anyone would be seen there, and "sleepy eyes told no tales."

You would see ballers and well known professional man there, walking in with his mistress, or their lover and sexual encounter for the night, sexual origin and desires didn't matter for that one night at the Ménage A' Trois because every fantasies came true. Each clientele would secure a bodyguard to escort them to their right to privacy, in their secret room, and every room was set up different to caters to a different fetish and fantasy. Some was set up like dungeon for mastery, bondage, and S & M participation; other was set up for other erotic pleasures.

Crystal and her ladies was temptation that lit the spark to every man and women's wildest desires.

* * * *

"It's a Get, Got Game Out There"

As the club began to grow, Victor focused on a different money making scheme that he was more familiar with. With his expertise he found his self traveling all over the world to make connections with other business men who needed to be smuggle out of their country into the US. These public official were about to be arrested in their county for embezzlement and if found guilty they and their whole family would be executed. Some left their family behind to face the consequences alone because the cost to smuggle out a whole family was much more then expected. Each head had a price of two hundred thousand dollars on it. So a family of five would be one million dollars US currency, plus the one million dollars, escort fee for shipping out of the county. When arriving into the United State by cargo freight, they would be met my a black

Yukon Denali truck that pulled up to the cargo hole and unload the passage into the back set of the vehicle, which was reinforced resembling a coffin with cushion padding on top to cover a back set for comfort, the measurement were five by six in diameter. Two people like a husband and wife, or three children, could be squeezed in tightly and would have enough oxygen to survive for approximately 90 minutes because of the small air hole that were cut into the sides of the box. With that measurement Victor was able to smuggle family members weighing under a hundred and fifty pounds each and a total of two hundred pounds maximum when transporting them across the boarder. The vehicle trunk was filled with junk items so if the vehicle was search and the trunk opened it would not be reveled that any one was being hiding inside.

Victor's expert knowledge in intelligence provide him with the ability to provide them with a fictitious passports, transportation and laundering of their cash into US dollars. His connections throughout the world gave him a free hand in setting up bank accounts overseas under his client's fictitious name.

When arriving in the US, Victor was able to set them up in a mansion, property brought for them under their new name. The mansion came with servants, and bodyguards around the clock "in the fashion they were accustom to," all for three million US dollars. Everything that they left behind was smuggled out and set-up under their fictitious name, so to be honest, they didn't leave anything behind, thanks to Victor.

Victor got a phone call one evening after he got back from one of his trips.

"Hello!"

"Is this Simon?" Simon was Victor's code name that he gave to his clients, in case they were caught and would not be able to give out any information that the authorities could use against him.

"Who wants to know?"

"My name isn't important right now!"

"How did you get my personal number?"

"We have a mutual friend; he gave me your number and said I should call you?"

"What about?" Victor was a little paranoid because only his clients were given his personal number only thru there passage into the US, after that they were never to contact him again, not for any reason.

"I would like to meet with you to discuss business." The strange voice on the phone said.

"Where at?"

"The train station."

"Why there?" Victor asked.

"Because I'll be coming in on the 187 west bound into Los Angeles, and I'll be leaving right out after our business is completed."

"Look if you think that you're gonna set me up to kill me in a public place and high-tail it out of here its not gonna happen!"

"It's not a set up, trust me! Tomorrow 12 noon, 187 west bound Los Angeles train station. I'll be wearing a L.A. Clippers blue ball cap."

(Click)

He hung-up! Victor was puzzled, he thought to himself, "I'll need Jordan with me on this one, he could be my eyes in case anything goes wrong."

Victor called Jordan that morning, "Hey man, I didn't know you were back in town. Are you coming down to the club? Crystal made some great improvements, and hired three new girls who will make your dick stand up and salute when you see them!"

"Yea sure, but first I need you to do me a favor!"

"Sure man anything, what is it?"

"I don't want to talk over the phone, so meet me at the little cafe on First and Broadway, park in the underground parking lot."

"What time?"

"10:30 and don't be late, and bring your guard dog! (click)

Jordan walked over to Crystal who was going through the dance routine with the new girls.

"Baby, come here!"

Jordan pulled Crystal to the side and started whispering in her ear, "I just spoke to Victor something up, he wouldn't explain it over the phone but he asked me to meet him in downtown Los Angeles at the little cafe on First and Broadway, but he was very adamant about me being on time, and being strapped."

"What time did he say?"

"10:30 this morning."

"I know Victor he wouldn't ask me to meet him unless he felt something was gonna happened and he needed me to watch his back.

"You better go, its 9:30 now and you know how bad traffic is trying to get into downtown Los Angeles, call me if anything goes wrong!" With that Crystal kissed Jordan on his lips and said, "Be careful..!"

Jordan had no problem with watching Victor's back. Jordan's piece of the club was for him to oversee all bodyguards and to hirer only the most loyal, the ones that would take a bullet before giving up or running away.

Chapter 2

"Behold a Dark Stranger"

It was 12 noon exactly when the bell tower struck twelve. Suddenly, out step a tall elderly man walking with a slight limp, he was wearing a blue Clippers ball cap and a dark trench coat like he was trying to conceal a weapon or something, he had on dark sunglasses and as he walked the limp became more noticeable. He began approaching Victor and as Victor notice the man walking toward him he realized that this man was physically fit for his age and his weigh was approximately 280 pounds and he stood at least 6' 2". His tall strong physique made it noticeable to victor that if he had to fight him he would need help from Jordan. Jordan who had station himself on the second story level looking down, was able to view everyone coming and going, and from Jordan's point of view the stranger appeared to be alone as he approached Victor and said, "Simon, are you him?"

Victor looked him in the eyes and replied, "Yes, I'm Simon."

The tall dark stranger said, "Let's go sit down over here where it's private."

Victor followed him but was very paranoid, as he walked beside him. Victor looked up to the second story platform to make sure that Jordan was still there watching everything that was going on. Jordan had his 45 automatic aimed at the stranger if anything went wrong and Victor gave the signal.

"Do you know who I am?" The stranger asked.

"No I don't, should I? What so important that you wanted to meet me here" Victor replied in a suspicious voice.

"Big Dog, isn't that your code name?"

"How do you know that"?

"I was overseas when you were there on your last assignment. I saw you and I knew right then who you were!"

"So you follow me all the way to the US, just to tell me that, what is this black mail?"

"No, I just had to see you and tell you the truth."

"Now you're really freaking me out..! What do you want?"

"Look at me...!"

Victor took a deep look into the tall stranger eyes.

I'm your Uncle!!! Your mother's brother, my name is Ruben!

"You can't be my Uncle! My mother didn't have any family except her parents who disowned her when she married my father and came to live in the United States."

"You're wrong; I'm her brother the one no one talks about, the black sheep of the family. When I saw you in Kosovo, I knew right then who you were! You looked so much like her before she left. That's when I followed you and heard you speaking to some public official, bribing them to look the other way. I came to warn you that those same men are the ones that are coming to the United States to kill you. One of them said, 'that you have too much power and know too much about them in their county, and if they continue to let you live there whole operation in public office will be ruined.'"

"How can they do anything to me?"

"Like you, they have connections here too, and they mentioned Las Vegas. I don't know what that means but it didn't sound good. You are my nephew, my sister's son. You and me are alike, black sheep's of our family. I can not stay any longer because I would put you in danger. Watch your back, if it is meant for us to meet again it will happen, may Allah be with you my brother!"

Just that quickly the tall dark stranger was gone. Jordan raced downstairs and ran over to where Victor was standing, panting and out of breath Jordan asked, "Who was he and what was that all about? Did he threaten you, or offer you money or what??? Say something, don't just stand there."

"He said that he was my Uncle on my mother's side, and that he saw me in Kosovo when I was there. He had overheard a plot to kill me from a high official that I do business with. He said they're afraid that I'm a threat to their business operation, he overheard them say that I know too much."

"Well are you?"

"What?" Victor replied in a daze.

"A threat to they're business operation?"

"NO, hell no!"

"Yea, but they think so... So what are we going to do?" Jordan asked.

"My Uncle Ruben mentioned that he heard them say something about Las Vegas."

"Las Vegas???"

"Yes, I said to him that it was no way in hell that they could get me here, and he said they have connections in Las Vegas."

"Those muthafuckas' will have to go thru me first before they get to you, and that's a promise!" Jordan's anger resonated in Victor's ears to reassure him!

* * * *

"A Toast to the Sweet life"

Ménage A' Trois was rolling in dough. Crystal took pride in being in charge of the girls. To advertise the club Crystal bought a brand new Cadillac Limousine, with a convertible top.   The color of the Cadillac was Champagne pink, with white leather upholstery. Crystal had her personal bodyguard chauffeur all the girls around town each Thursday night to promote Friday, Saturday and Sunday's performance. Each night was a different theme. Friday was sizzling hot momma's night. The girls would one by one perform on stage wearing a sizzling hot g-string, tassel nipples, sheer lace stocking, gloves, and six inch Stiletto heels. On Saturday it was anything goes night, and the girls would walk out either naked, but cleverly revealing their self with lights, beaming off them as they slide around the pole, and slithered on the marble stage. Sunday, was the finale were Crystal draped herself in nothing but jewelry from head to toe. And one by one she would remove the jewelry as she revealed her beautiful voluptuous body. Her curved hips, and full round butt and nipples reaching out to all the horny men, temping them into full masturbation. Her wealthy clientele drooled and screamed with passion in their voice that only Crystal could cause an erection. Her sexuality came full blown when she inserted her middle finger in her pussy and started groaning and panting with passion, delighting her self and saying to each clientele in the audience, "Don't you wish you could have a taste of this delicious wet pussy?" By the end of her performance the audience would go wild removing watches, and diamond rings, and any jewelry that they had on and throw it on stage. And when that was gone they pulled out their wallets with money and credit cards in it and everything was thrown at her feet. Crystal's beauty was spellbinding, and to look at her you would give up all your worldly possessions to be able to lust in her presence.

After Crystal performance all the items that were thrown on stage, was brought to her dressing room and Crystal would place all the items in a safe and sort through them the next day. Crystal was tired after each performance because she put so much energy into her work. She'd think to herself, "it's not easy being this sexy and beautiful!" Jordan and Victor walked into her dressing room, "hi babe tired?" Jordan said removing her six inch stiletto heels off her feet and rubbing them.

"Yes,"

"They loved you tonight out there, you know that don't you?" Victor added.

"I know they love me every night. I'm a bitch hard to resist!"

"What are you going to do with all this stuff?" Victor asked. Picking up one of the wallets and thumbing through it.

"Go through it tomorrow and take out all the money from the wallets and hock the jewelry." Crystal said.

"You really laid it on them tonight, made me wanna' fuck you! Look at these fools." Victor said picking up one of the wallets and reading off the name on driver's license, "William Van-Eddy." Victor read.

"Who? What did you say? Crystal voice got shaky.

"William Van-Eddy, someone you know?" Victor asked.

Jordan stopped rubbing Crystal feet as she jumped up to grab the wallet from Victor's hand.

"No I didn't know him if I did he wouldn't have been able to fuck over me like he did..!"

"What is it baby-girl, what happened?" Jordan asked as he put his arm around Crystal holding her in his strong arms to comfort her.

"He's the muthafucka that raped me and pulled a train on me in college and got away with it, him and all his so called friends. I always told myself that if I ever saw him again his ass would be mines. Now this son of a bitch pop's up in my club...!"

"So what are we going to do about it?" Victor didn't give a second thought to getting even with him.

"He's my problem, I'll handle it myself!"

"Baby-girl, we got your back...!"

"I told you I can handle it!" Crystal snapped at Jordan in a loud aggressive voice.

"Ok, ok...! Settle down! It's me baby the one who love's you and would do anything for you!" Jordan walked over to Crystal and began hugging her tightly, Crystal's heart was beating fast at the remembrance of what happened so long ago, it was as if it happened yesterday to her, those feeling of helplessness never left her, feelings that she never wanted to feel ever again. But now, here they were surfacing up again, a ugly gorilla on her back, pulling her down that road again.

"I'll handle it! Don't worry about me I'll be ok!" Crystal said.

* * * *

"Up Pops a Weasel"

Willie Van Eddy had become one of the most prestigious players on the NFL team. He married the daughter of a Senator from New Jersey, while playing for the New York Jets. But, because of his reputation with the women his marriage was falling apart.

Willie was visiting the coast and was ballin' hard and he would pick up women and party all night drinking Grand Marnier Tequila shots and snoring cocaine, he asked his limousine driver where the best club in town was, and the driver said, "None other then the Ménage A' Trois in Beverly Hills."

"Ok, let's turn this love bus around and go!" Willie said.

Willie stumble in with his entourage of co-players some lady-friends and two bodyguards, and they all were juiced up and speeding.

As the music began to play Crystal came out seductively dancing, her body moving back and forth to the beat of the music. Willie didn't recognize her because in college she was just a girl, now she had evolved into a goddess of lust, seducing every man's fantasy and capturing every man's dream, and at the same time becoming every married women's nightmare. Willie was mesmerized when he saw her on stage, all his sexual desires came flowing out of him and he came right there in his pants. Crystal exited her performance to the rear of the stage and all the men in the audience went wild. That was when Willie took off his Movado watch and threw it on stage, then he removed his NFL ring, and threw that on stage, finally he took his wallet out of his back pocket that had twenty-seven hundred dollars in it and threw that on stage, with everything in it, his driver's license, two major credit cards, pictures of his wife, three kids and his dog.

Willie's life was headed down hill; he was being brought up on charges for point shaving. He was put on suspension without pay until a full investigation could be completed. His family was so discussed in him that his wife threw him out of the house and his parents refused to speak to him. So what's a nigga to do? Leave town and spend more money on women, drugs and liquor, high-rolling and flossing, and that's what Willie did.

* * * *

"Count-Down"

Crystal sat all alone in her penthouse suite in Beverly Hills with Willies' wallet in her hand. She sat there rubbing the leather of his wallet with her thumb in one hand and holding his driver's license in the other. Her mind shifted back and forth between years, now and what happened then. She couldn't stop thinking, her mind was racing inside her head like the seductive beat that she danced off of. Each beat aroused more and more in her the memory of that night that she found herself alone and naked in that dirty motel room after being raped. The tears began to flow down her cheeks, "What did I do to him to deserve that?" She asked herself, but there wasn't an answer!"

Crystal looked down at the address on the license, is there a phone number? She thumbed though the wallet again. "Here's a business card! William Van-Eddy, Executive Manager for Public Affairs. So what this muthafucka has a business card for his affairs to fuck around? This son of bitch gonna get what he has coming to him!"

Crystal dialed the number on the card, 213-333-5521.

"Hello, Mr. Van-Eddy's office, may I help you?"

"Hello, I'd like to speak to Mr. Van-Eddy..!"

"Who shell I say is calling?"

"A Good Samaritan, I found something that belongs to him and I'd like to return it."

"One moment please!"

"Mr. Van-Eddy speaking, how can I help you?"

"Well Mr. Eddy, I found something that belongs to you and I'd like to return it?" Crystal said in a sultry voice.

"You do say?" Willies voice became intrigued with the sound of her sexy voice on the other end of the phone.

"Can I met you some place?" Crystal voice sounded so sexy over the phone that Willie's curiosity was getting the better of him.

"Sure, but what is it that you'd like to return?"

"Your wallet, but the money gone, I spent it on something special for you, so I'd like to repay you for it."

"My wallet, I remember where I lost it, so you're the person that found it?"

"Yes..!"

Willie's jumped up as his dick got hard all over again, when he realize who it was. "Where can we met?" Willie asked.

"I know somewhere that's private and no one will disturb us, the Sunset Inn, in Inglewood, ten o'clock, room 313, I'll see you there!" (click) Crystal said as she hung up and smiled a devious smile.

"Willie's thought to himself, "this bitch don't know what she's about to get, my dick is so hard it could bust rocks right now. I wanted to hit that ass last night but I fucked up. That bitch has that sexy erotic pussy that can reach out and touch a nigga with out laying a hand on him." Willie started bustin' up to himself at the thought of it.

* * * *

"Beware Of the Bird That Sings At Night"

Crystal arrived at nine o'clock that evening at the Sunset Motel. She got there early on purpose to get everything ready for a night Willie would never forget. She stopped by the liquor store and brought a bottle of Johnny Walker Black Label Scotch and two paper cups. Then she stopped by an erotic sex store in the area and purchased some sex toys, some handcuffs, wipes, gloves, and a few surprises for him. She scented the room with her perfume to cover over the dingy smell of the motel room. Then she deemed the lights and waited for him. Her cell phone rung, "Hello, Ok that's good I'll call you back when I'm ready! (Click)

Crystal heart was beating so fast, she took a shot of the Scotch to calm her nerves.

9:30 p.m.

9:45 p.m. the clock was ticking away slowly. Crystal took another shot of Scotch.

9:55 p.m. Then a knock at the door.

"Come in it's open!"

Crystal was setting up on the bed with a black leather fitting cat-suit that complimented her full body skin tight. She was wearing black six inch boots that came up to her thighs and as the door swung open she was looking him dead in his face. Crystal gained control of herself fast before she did something stupid, like jumping up and stomping his ass to death with those six inch boots she was wearing.

"Well I'd never thought I'd be meeting you here, if you'd like we could go somewhere else a little nicer then this place!" Willie said.

"No this suits me just fine," Crystal said in a sexy voice.

Crystal got up and walked over to him, and began unbuttoning his shirt and removing his jacket. Willie just stood there with his dick erect bulging out of his pants. Then Crystal started unbuttoning his pants and unzipping them.

"Hold on baby!"

"What you're not sure if you want this pussy?"

"Sure I do, hell yea..! But slow down before I come, then you'd have to exercise your mouth to get it back up!"

"Well let's see what tools I have to exercise with?"

Then she stood in front to him and pulled out his dick and started massaging it.

"Humm! And how does this big boy like it?"

"Rough and tough..!"

"Ok, lets have a drink to 'rough and tough'!"

Crystal walked over to the table where the liquor bottle was sitting and grabbed the cup that she hadn't drunk out of and poured Willie a double shot of Scotch and two ice cubes. Then she poured her self a shot in the cup that she had drunk out of earlier.

Willie sip it and said, "Wow baby this is some strong stuff."

Crystal down her shot, straight. "What you can't handle it? Should I add a little milk in yours?"

So Willie down his drink in one swallow.

"That's some strong shit..! Is it hot in here to you? Woo, I need some fresh air."

"I'll turn the air conditioner on for you." Crystal walked over to the window where the air conditioner was hooked-up to, and turned it on full blast, it was so old that it began making all kinds of loud noises.

"Say, why don't you lay down in the bed so that big dick of yours can wet my pussy up!"

Willie fell back on the bed butt naked, with is dick standing straight up at attention. Crystal just laugh with a sinister laugh, and reach for her purse that was on the night stand and took out the handcuffs and handcuffed Willie's right and left hand to the bed, his legs she tided with a cord around his ankles. Willie's head was spinning, and his eye sight was blurred, unaware that his drink was laced with ecstasy the same drug that he had used on Crystal. He began shouting, "what's going on? What are you doing?"

Crystal stood in front of the bed and said, "You don't remember me do you? I was the one that you and your so called friends raped and left me in that scumbag motel like trash after each of you were through raping me. I stayed in the hospital for three days and no charges was every filed against you and your friends because your family was some big shots in the community. I lost my scholarship, my dignity, and my self respect. But I swore that if I ever had the chance to get even, you would pay."

"I'm sorry, we were just drunk having fun, just having fun!" Willie's voice began to fade out as he fell in and out of consciousness.

"Wake up you son of a bitch, it's not going to be that easy for you, you're going to know how it feels to be fucked over and can't do any thing about it."

Then Crystal picked up her cell phone and made a call. "Yeah, come-on now!"

Crystal had been looking out-of the curtains through the windows when she opened the door and four of her big buff bodyguards came walking in..!

"He's all your, I want you fuck him every which way and when your finish with him, kill him!"

Willie who was conscience enough to know what was about to happen began to scream, but the sounds of the air conditioner only drowned-out the screams.

Crystal walked over to him laying in the bed and with one sharp swoop of a straight razor she sliced his dick off, and as he let out a loud scream she stuffed it in his mouth and said, "You won't be needing this any more." And walked out!

Chapter 4

"Check and Double Check"

Victor didn't take it seriously about what his uncle told him. Him, Jordan, and Crystal discussed the conversation that he had with his uncle but they all agreed that they had enough protection, bodyguards and ammunition to hold off an army if they had to. Victor special forces in the Marines, and Jordan fighting technique and skills, and Crystal ability to recognize a dirty muthafucka a mile away was good enough, all three felt that if any thing went down then they would be able to handle it.

Jordan who was in charge of the bodyguards put each of them on alert. They were to carry their guns on them at all times. And if they suspect some-one, then they were to signal him as soon as possible and everything would be on lock down. Jordan had hired extra bodyguards to fill in around the clock.

One of the bodyguards that Jordan hired was name Sal. Sal showed his self to be willing to work extra hours, chauffeur Crystal around town on his day off and he never caused any trouble with the other bodyguards. There were times when the male testosterone would flare up over one of the beautiful women that they had to chauffeur around town, and most of the time a fight would brake out and before you know it Jordan would have to step in and lay both of them out, with a quick left cross to the jaw on one and a right upper cut to the stomach on the other. But, Sal was different, he was a nice enough guy, but there was something mysterious about him. He was too perfect, too helpful, always sticking around after everyone else had gone home, always peeping over your shoulder when you would be opening your mail, or his shifty eye movement trying to read the business letters that were on your desk. Victor noticed it first, each time Victor went to make a buy, or send a shipment; Sal would volunteer to drive him. Even though Victor had intentions on driving his self, Sal would talk him into changing his mind. But, then something else strange began to happen, there shipment wasn't being delivered on time, and a large shipment of guns and high tech equipment that Victor would send out to his connections overseas was being stolen. When he mentioned it to Jordan, Jordan only said, "Man don't get all up-tight, shit happens!"

"I'm sure shit happens, but this shit's been happening for the last eight months. I'm gonna run a thorough back ground check on everyone that works for us, that includes' the girls and the bodyguards." Victor said.

"I already did and every one came out clean!" Jordan argued.

"Well I'm gonna run another one, you have a problem with that pretty boy!"

"Fuck you man, you're full of shit..!" Jordan said.

Crystal who was sitting there listing to the whole conversation knew that Victor was right. When Victor suspected something is wrong, nine times out of ten he's right. "Listen little boys if you want to fight after schools out it's ok with me, but now it's time to find out what's going down and stop it before it shuts us down."

"I still have friends in secret intelligence, I'll give one a call and fax over our list of employees who are working under us, also the company and their people that we've been dining with. Maybe it's an inside job and someone's trying to get over on us."

"There you go again, jumping to conclusions. We've been doing business with those companies for over five years, so why now all of a sudden they'd try to jack us?" Jordan asked.

"I don't know, but if it's not one of them it's here in our own household, and that's a No, No!" Victor wasn't playing when he said that, NO ONE crossed him!

* * * *

"What Goes Around Comes Around"

"So what did you find out on the identification report?" Crystal asked.

"I'm not sure, but I think we have a mole among us."

"Who?"

Just then there was a knock at the door. "Who is it?"

"It's me Jordan."

"Come in man, why the fuck are you knocking?"

"I found someone outside the door! Sal..!"

"Yes, hello Mr. Victor, I wanted to ask if you need me to drive you anywhere today. I'm off today and I didn't have anything to do, so I thought I could do some extra work around the club!" Sal said.

"Not today Sal go home!"

"It's no problem Mr. Victor I could mop-up around here or empty the trash!"

"I said, Go Home!"

"Yes Sir Mr. Victor, right away!"

"Man why the fuck did you talk shit to him like that Victor, he only wants to help around here, the other bodyguards just do their shift and leave at less Sal's willing to work extra hours around here!"

"Jordan, look at this!"

"What is it?"

"I was just about to show Crystal when you knocked on the door. Sal might have been trying to listen in through the door..!"

"Why the fuck would he do something like that for?"

"His name is on this list, he's not who he says he is!"

Jordan pick-up the list and began reading what it said about Sal. "This has to be wrong, I checked him out my self and he cleared!"

"Well according to secret intelligence his real name is Saleme and he's from Las Vegas not San Francisco. His family is part of the cartel that runs most of the gambling houses down there that are not connected to the big casino. His grandfather migrated from Kosovo, 40 years ago and still has a hand in some of the dirty laundering of cash that flows through there. My uncle Ruben mentioned that a Las Vegas Mafia Kingpin took notice of the Ménage A' Trois and wants our business and will not stop at nothing to get it, even to go as far as blowing the place up if he can't have it."

"And you think Sal's the mole?" Jordan's sounded a little confused about the whole deal. He hired Sal personally and took him under his wing to show him the ropes. If Sal was playing him for a chump, then there's gonna be some reckoning to be had.

"Jordan, Victor both of you, let's just watch him and see what happens. Lets' set up a false shipment and have him drive you to the port when you send it off. Have him wait out by the car and don't let him go inside with you, then Jordan you follow them and stay out of sight, use one of the girls car so you're not noticed, and when Victor goes inside without him see what Sal does." Crystal idea made a lot of sense...!

"Brains and beauty, you're my type of women. But you're right baby-girl; let's find out for sure if he's our mole before we go half cock with this. Speaking of cock, maybe you could rub mines for a while and relieve some of this stress from my dick?"

"Shut-up Jordan, you could be a little more romantic about asking me to fuck you, don't you think?"

"Hey babe, I'm just keeping it real with you! Look baby-girl, if I'm gonna ask you for some pussy it won't be around this crazy ass nigga! I'ma wait until he's no where around so that he won't come knocking on the door trying to peep in!" Jordan said as they all started bustin' up.

* * * *

"Beware of a Kiss Ass!"

It was eleven o'clock Thursday evening, Victor gathered together some phony shit to have packed and ready for shipment. Sal wasn't aloud to follow Victor into the warehouse, but to keep him off track Victor had him stand by the door and not to let any one in. Sal took a guards position out side the door, with his ear listening through the crack. Two hours later Victor came out with three crates being pushed by two workers.

"You ready to go boss? Where we going down to the harbor?" Sal asked.

"Stop asking so many questions, just help put those crates in the back of the truck and shut the fuck up and drive. Take the 710 freeway, I'll tell you where to get off.

Watch the speed limit; I don't wanna get stopped by no fucken cops!"

"Yes boss!"

Victor was sure that at some point Sal would show his hand, so he was ready. He had his 44 revolver tuck away in a shoulder holster under his jacket.

As they drove onto the 710 freeway, Jordan trail from behind being careful not to be spotted in Sal rear view mirror.

They arrived at the pier in Terminal Island, and pulled up to dock 357. Several big tankers were dock there, one man that spoke with an accent walked over to Victor and shook his hand, then two men walked from behind the tanker and Victor told Sal to open the back of the truck. Sal opened it and the two buff looking rustic men grabbed the crates and carried them inside to the rear of the tanker.

"Wait here by the truck and don't follow!" Victor instructed Sal.

"Yes boss!"

Jordan just arrived a few minutes later, and drove up to the pier with his head lights off, from where he was park he had a clear view of Sal, who seemed very nerves. He lit one cigarette and smoked it, then lit another and threw it down, then suddenly Jordan heard a cell phone ring. Sal answered it.

"Yeah he's inside!   I don't know, I can't see nothin' from out here! I can't, he said for me to wait by the car. Ok, ok, I'll try and take a look!" Sal ran behind to the back where Victor and the other man took the crates. Jordan followed him from behind, being careful not to make a sound, and from the light beaming from the top of the yard pole where the tankers were stored for shipment, Jordan was able to watch Sal continue talking to the other person on his cell phone.

"Ok, I could see them now, there's about a couple of million on the table, yea he's counting it. There must be something very valuable in those crates to pay that much for it!" Sal whispered on the phone. "They're putting it in the bag, I gotta' get back to the truck. It's here Dock 357,

Terminal Island.... I gotta go!" Sal hung up and ran back to the truck.

Jordan heard everything! He just didn't know who Sal was talking to on the other end of the phone!

Victor walked back to the truck with a large bag in his hand and Sal was standing there. Victor got in the back seat of the truck and said, "Drive off!"

"Where to boss?"

"It don't matter just drive!"

"Yes, boss!"

Victor waited for Jordan's call. But, Jordan walked back to the tankers to talk to the Captain of the ship who Victor had delivered the crates.

"Hi my friend, I knew you had to be close by. My Vikta' would never do anything without his right-hand man covering his back!"

"Yes, we got our mole. He made a phone call and was telling them everything that went down, his fucken goons are on their way down here! Are you and your men ready for them?"

"Yes, my friend...! But, how many are there?"

124

"I don't know, but I want you to let them steal the crates because we need to know who these muthafuckas are and who they work for. Also, I don't want you and your men getting shot-up over some phony shit. You're too valuable to us alive!"

"No problem my friend, but if you need us to kill them we're ready now..! Me and my men haven't killed someone for weeks, and we're ready to put in some work!"

"No just let them steal the crates, and I'll following them from behind when they leave!"

The captain and his two workers moved from where the crates were stored to the connecting room in the rear where they would be able to watch everything that was about to happened.

Six men all carrying automatic machine guns enter the rear of the tanker ship wearing hooded ski mask and entered in exactly were the crates were being stored and began to carry them out without any disturbance. The captain and his men watched quietly without making a sound. Jordan who had stationed himself in front on the top of the tankers watched them load the crates into a plain cab truck, and then they pull away with their lights off down the path that lead onto the highway with Jordan following.

"Victor's cell rung"

"Yeah Vic our man's dirty, his fucken friends arrived right after you pulled off. They loaded the crates and they got on the 710 freeway. I'm following them now. They're carrying the crates in a plain truck, I don't know where there headed but I'll let you know."

(click)

"Everything ok boss?" Sal asked.

"Head back to the club; I have some unfinished business there."

Sal got on the 101 freeway and headed for the club, without asking any more questions.

"Hay babe I'm headed to the club now, who's on duty? Ok have all four of them met me when we pull up! Make sure, everyone else is gone. I'll be there in an hour, stay sweet for me!"

Crystal know that something was about to go down, so she had the bodyguards that were on duty to stand ready on guard waiting for Victor to arrive at the rear entrance with Sal driving him.

Sal got paranoid with Victor's call to Crystal, he had a hunch that something had gone wrong. "Boss, I need to pull over for a minute the tire on the divers side don't sound good. I think we pick up a nail when we stopped back there. I can pull-up in that gas station off the freeway, ok boss?"

"No don't stop, it'll be ok. Just get back to the club!" Victor order in a stern voice..!

"Boss I really think we should stop!"

"I said NO, you fucken ass hole, just drive!"

With that Victor pulled out his 44 automatic and aimed for Sal's head and fired off a shot, Sal ducked and the bullet went through the windshield of the truck and shattered the front glass. Sal, reached around and tried to grab the gun from Victor's hand, but Victor was to quick and shot Sal with two shots, one in the neck and the other in the chest. Sal hunched over the seat of the truck while Victor braced himself as the truck lost control and ran right into a steal pole.

"What the fuck, this son of a bitch won't tell us shit now!" Victor thought to himself as he got out of the truck, just then his cell phone rung.

"Yea, Jordan..! Where are you?"

"I'm on highway 15 headed for Vegas!"

"Stay on them; I had to put our man down. So you have our only lead. Call me when you get there!"

Victor called Crystal.

"Hay baby girl, I need you to send Roscoe and Roland to pick me up in the moving truck. I can't talk now...I'll tell you every thing later! Babe shut the fuck-up and JUST DO AS I SAID! And don't argue with me. I need them here now! Right off highway 101, about ten minutes from the club, tell them to look for my black Yukon truck smashed round a steal pole. Hurry up before the cops come. Our man took two shots trying to be brave!" (click)

Victor grabbed Sal's body and dragged it into a vacant lot, just in case the police arrived before Roscoe and Roland got there.

"Time to Get the Hell Out of Here"

Jordan was getting a little sleepy when the truck pulled off the freeway and it arrived at State Line. The truck exited the main highway and turned left onto a side street and came to the front gate of an abandon casino. Jordan was unable to follow through the front gate so he drove around to the side and parked, then he hopped over a fence and ran across the yard to the loading docks were he watched the crates being unloaded. That's when he saw him! A well dress heavy set man about seventy years old, walking with a limp came out from behind the shadows in the corner and order the flunkies that were carrying the crates to open them. One ran and got a crowbar and with one hard pop of the crate it opened. Then he did the same to the next wooden slate and it popped open. Searching through the crate he found nothing but bars of bricks, then he walked over to the next one, and they found the same thing... bars of bricks!

"What is this, a JOKE? Where are the guns?"

"I don't know Sir!!!" One of the flunkies's answered.

"Saleme said that something valuable was in there."

"Call Saleme, call him!!!"

"I tried calling him Sir, but no answer..!"

"Something wrong, head back to Los Angeles and find Saleme, we're hitting the club tonight, and taking everything, their business, money, and most of all the women Crystal..! Call everyone in the area, and no one fucks-up or they'll have to answer to me!"

Jordan knew that it was time for him to get the hell out of there, he jump off the loading dock and ran across the yard, hopped over the fence and back to his car. Aah! Shit I forgot to call Victor, "Hay Vic this shit is bigger then we thought, some fat muthafucka with a limp is getting all his flunkies together to hit our shit back home tonight! I just heard them talking so I'm getting the hell out of here and back home to be there when the shit hit the fan."

"No, fuck that, shot the fat muthafucka now so he won't be able to reach our shit at home!"

"Are you crazy? I'm not going back in there and try to end this on my own!"

"Man just shot the fat muthafucka, he's the boss the rest will not follow. I know that for sure J', I'd use this in military strategy in my field combat operations, trust me, it works!" (click)

"Damn, now he's got me going back in there after I done made a clean getaway. I must be the fool in this relationship."

Jordan hopped back over the fence and jumped up onto the loading dock and looked back into the window, no one was there. "Where the fuck are they?" Just then the fat muthafucken boss came walking back through there with two henchmen on each side. "Damn I'ma have to shot all three of them, which one first, I better aim for the middle cause that fat muthafucken target I can't miss."

Jordan took aim then as soon as Jordan shot the muthafucken boss who was standing in the middle decided to sit down in a chair that was behind him and Jordan missed, and before he realized what happened bullets were flying all around him. "Why'd that fat lazy muthafucka had to set down just then?" Jordan thought to himself as he jumped off the loading docks and ran across the yard where two big goon bodyguards took off running after him shooting. Jordan hopped over the fence and ran to his car and punched it down the road hitting the highway doing 110 mph down State Line. But not soon enough, those same goons were on him like flies to shit. But Jordan's Dodge Challenger RT was no match for them and before he knew it he had put miles between him and them. With all that running and shooting Jordan didn't realize that he had been shot, just a surface wound but it was bleeding bad. Jordan grabbed his coat that was next to him in the passage seat and pressed it tightly against his side as he took off down highway 15.

Jordan wound was beginning to hurt after the adrenaline had worn off from the shooting. He started to nod off as he drove down the highway. If he didn't pull over soon he might find his self on the side of the road. Jordan started seeing lights in the distance faster and faster

Jordan drove as the lines in the center divider started floating by like a roller coaster ride. Finally there it was a gas station in the middle of no where. Jordan pulled over and parked in back where all the big rigs traveling across country parked and the driver's rested before heading back onto the highway.

"You have a restroom in here?" Jordan asked the casher.

Jordan was still holding his side with his coat balled up and his arm holding it.

"I'll take these, how much?" Jordan had grabbed some duck tape, Kotex pads, alcohol and Advil and carried it into the restroom.

Jordan was really feeling the pain now, with his past habit of snorting cocaine he swear he'd never do it again but he would keep some in his pocket for his women who did. He opened up the small bag of coke that he had with him, and poured a little out on the back of his hand, and then he snorted it hard into his nostrils. Bang!!! He snorted a little more, bang, bang!!! He was feeling no more pain, and his head was floating on cloud nine! He cleaned off his wound with alcohol, and placed the Kotex's pads on the wound to soak-up the blood then he ripped off a piece of duck tape and wrapped it around his side tightly to stop the bleeding, then Jordan opened the bottle of Advil and swallowed a few.

Jordan walked back out around to his car but he knew driving another four hours would be impossible.

"Yo my brother, are you ok?" A voice from behind Jordan asked.

"Yea, man I'm fine."

"Yo man you don't look fine. Are you about to drive some where? Because I've been driving long enough to have seen to many accident on this highway to know you're not going to make it. Let me give you a ride, so you can rest. I'm not trying to scam on you asked inside I come through here once a week, I got a wife and kids that I love, I don't want them to find me spread across this highway because some fool decided to get in his car and drive! You feel me?"

"Yeah man, I feel you!"

So, where you headed?"

"L.A."

"That's where I'm headed, hop in!"

"Ok.. but first I'ma make a phone call."

"Yo beautiful where's Vic?"

"Jordan where are you?"

"I'm ok; I'm hitching a ride with a truck driver. What's your name? Cosmo! Cosmo yeah? Now listen baby girl, if I don't make it back within four hours I was last scene in a large trailer truck license plate number 649SVD741, heading into L.A. Remember that, no write it down, no telling, this muthafucka could be some wanted serial killer, and I'm his next victim." Jordan said as he started bustin' up!

"What's wrong with you baby?"

"Naw baby girl, I'm just a little fucked-up. Let Vic know that I took a bullet for him listening to his advice, now my shit is fucked up! Also Candy's car is parked at the Last Fill-Up gas station on highway 15 parked in the rear, don't forget to have someone come and pick it up for me and drive it back to the club, the key is under the mat in the front seat!"

"You are too crazy boy, let me go I'll hold things down until you get here, love you baby-boy!"

(click)

"Ok Cosmo my man, let's roll..!

Chapter 5

"Watch Your Back"

It was Saturday night and the girls are schedule to perform in their naughty girl routine wearing their sexiest naughty girl custom.

"Cinnamon I need you to come out to center stage because there'll be some special VIP's arriving and I'll finish off with the finale. Candy you take stage left."

"Un un Crystal I'm not following up behind her." Candy bitched.

"I'm the back-up for center stage, not her with her bony ass!"

"Listen you little haffa' you'll do as I say or you'll get your shit and get the hell out of here! Do you think I have the time to put-up with you're PMS? I have bigger shit to deal with! So get your costume on and do as I said..!"

"But Crystal, I'm just saying!!"

"What?? I told you what to do Candy now do it before I put my foot in your ass!"

"Bitch you better watch your back!" Candy said to Cinnamon!

"You and what other bitch?" Cinnamon said as she just turned and walked away.

It's was nine o'clock and the club was filled with rich and famous clientele. Cinnamon came out center staged and the club went wild, she sashayed in her long see-through silk red rob that opened-up down the front and revealed her firm breast, and her heart shape pussy hair line with nothing else underneath. As she circle and turned and teased the crowd by making love to the pole and wrapping her leg around it twirling around as if it was a large hard dick. Her sultry voice sounds of moaning and groaning only stimulated the audience even more.

Then Candy walked out stage left, in a short baby-doll see-though button down gold nighty. She sashayed around the pole as if she owned the stage, and the crowd began to throw money on stage. Candy looked over at Cinnamon, and rolled her eyes. Candy bent over showing her big butt to the audience legs spread apart to reveal her clean shaved pussy that teased and tantalized the crowd while she switched her fat sexy ass on stage.

Next from stage right Luscious came walking out in her six inch black stiletto heels. She was wearing a black lace see-through cat women suit, with a perfect 38x 24x 40x shape that left nothing for the imagination. She sashayed around and around the pole then slither down the pole onto the floor clawing on all fours, wiggling her fat ass in the audience face, each man in the club went wild..!

Then all three ladies formed a circle and began caressing the pole and licking it as if they were making love to it and each other. The bodyguards on duty did their best to control the men in the club. Then Crystal came popping up from the center covered in hundred dollar bills, and two silver dollars pasted to her nipples. Everyone in the club began throwing there money on stage as each lady formed a circle of love around Crystal and began rubbing and kissing her from head to toe as she began panting and breathing hard, and Cinnamon, Candy, and Luscious inserted their finger into her pussy, and then the stage curtain came down.

As the curtain fell, Victor arrived and was standing in the rear off stage, watching the clientele in the audience, when he notices a familiar face. His heart began beating fast as he put his hand on his 44 automatic that he had holstered up to his side. Crystal was in her dressing room when Victor knocked quietly on her door. Jake, Crystal's personal bodyguard was standing outside her dressing room, to stop any unwanted intruders from stocking her.

"Jake, who is it?" Crystal asked

"It's me baby, Victor!"

"Let him in Jake..!"

"Hi babe you made it back safely!"

"Yeah, just in time to catch your finale. You need to stop teasing our customers like that, before some one has a heart attack watching you masturbate!"

"What better place to drop dead then in here, where all your fantasy come true?" Crystal added.

"Listen baby girl, where's Jordan?"

"I got a call from him and he's on his way back, he had to hitch a ride in a big rig truck with some stranger, and he said if he's not back within four hours come looking for him, you know how crazy he gets sometime! Is something wrong?"

"Yes, I saw my uncle in the audience!"

"Your uncle?"

"Well he said he was my uncle. Remember I went to meet this caller at the train stations down town! It's him, he was the one who warned me about the kingpin from Vegas that wanted to take over our club, and every since then funning things have been happening. Sal was the mole; I had to put him down when he tried to attack me."

"I knew something was up with him. I never trusted him, he was too sneaky. Never trust a sneaky bald guy!" Crystal said.

"Yeah, he made a call from the docks while Jordan was watching my back, then Jordan stayed behind to see if anyone would show-up. They did and crept in with machine guns, and shit. We let them steal the crates without any incident to allow Jordan to follow them."

"What does that have to do with your uncle showing up here?"

"I don't know but the last thing that Jordan said to me when he arrived in Vegas was that there was a fat older man that walked with a limp that gave orders. I didn't put two and two together until just now!"

"You mean to say that it's him, your uncle and the Kingpin are one in the same?" Crystal found that hard to believe.

"What else! We'll know for sure when Jordan gets here."

Get the girls back on stage, and get the band to play another set. I don't want anyone leaving yet, until Jordan gets here. Call him and find out how soon he'll be here?

* * * *

"It's Not Over Until the Fat Lady Sings"

It was an hour later when Jordan arrived in a two ton big rig.

"Thanks man for the ride any time you're in town just stop by the club, everything's on the house for you."

"Is that right young bro, I'll be back in town next week I'll see you then, Cosmo said!"

Jordan jumped down from the big rig holding his side and went into the club from the rear entrance. Jake was still standing at Crystal dressing room door when Jordan came walking down the hall way.

"What's up my nigga?" Jordan asked.

Jake just rolled his eyes and looked down at Jordan holding his side, and opened the door for him and said, "everyone's inside waiting for you!"

"Jordan are you alright?" Crystal said as she noticed him holding his side tightly.

"Man you're bleeding!" Victor said.

"No shit! Those fucking goons shot me!"

"Who were they?"

"I don't know but some punk ass fat dude with a limp was calling the shots!'

"Jordan man, I need you to look up front in the VIP section and see if that fat muthafucka that was calling the shots is in here?"

"What..? Jordan jump up to his feet and looked through the way-one glass mirror that was shielding them from view of the audience.

"Yeah, that's that muthafucka!"

"Ok, that's that muthafucka that I met at the train station that said he was my uncle!"

"No shit, him? YOU'RE UNCLE?"

"Yeah, that's what he said..!! And that I should be aware of some kingpin from Las Vegas that will be moving in trying to take over our club and won't stop at nothing to get it! Victor added.

"Well let's kill the muthafucka here and now! He's in our club, we could tell the police that he slipped and fell and shot his self." Jordan said.

144

"Jordan that's not gonna work, he has too many of his goons around him!" Crystal replied.

"No, it will work, we could say that they slipped and fell and shot them selves too! Who knows as stupid as they look the police would probably believe it!"

"Jordan stop, they may look stupid but the police isn't!" Crystal laughed it off.

"Let's just wait and see what happens! Get all the bodyguards to stand posted at there position. I'm going out front." Victor said.

Victor walked out slowly from the front entrance of the stage with his 44 automatic concealed under his coat shoulder holster, and over to Uncle Ruben's table.

"Well Victa, I see you didn't take my advice!"

"Uncle Ruben what's going on?"

"DON'T call me that!"

"Uncle?"

"Yes, DON'T CALL ME THAT!!"

"Why not, you said you were my uncle on my mother side of the family."

"I LIED...!"

"You son of a bitch!" And with that Victor pulled out his 44 automatic and began firing at the so called Uncle Ruben a.k.a big time Kingpin from Las Vegas. Victor ducked as Ruben's bodyguard that was standing next to him let out a scream when he pull out his double barrel shot gun and aimed it at Victor. Victor's bodyguards that were on point shot back at Ruben's bodyguard that had the double barrel shot gun and dropped him with multiple shots. Jordan who had been watching from the one-way glass mirror began blasting through the mirror just in time to shoot down the tall muthafucka that was creeping up from behind Victor. Jordan jumped out of the broken glass mirror onto the stage and continued shooting repeated rounds after landing on his feet on stage and rolling onto the ground. Ruben's goons all started firing at Jordan as he crawled on the floor over to Victor, who was reloading his 44 automatic. Jordan was out of bullets when out of nowhere five of Ruben's goons stood up, and Ruben a.k.a Kingpin started laughing and shouting in a sinister voice, "So muthafuckas you thought I couldn't take this club away from you, huh? Ha, ha!! Say good bye to everything that was yours and hello to all that is mines now..!" As Kingpin Ruben's goon took aim to fire their guns into Victor and Jordan's body, just then Jake, Crystal personal bodyguard jump on top of Victor and Jordan shielding them with his body to protect them from gun fire. Jakes blood flowed from his body like water pouring out saving Victor and Jordan's life. As Ruben and his goons walked out of the shadows for the kill, out from Center stage came gun fire and running out blasting was Crystal with two of her girls, Candy and Luscious they were dress to kill, wearing six inch stilettos boots that tied around their thighs, and a black cat-women's one-piece outfit, with an under-arm shoulder holsters packing two 44 automatics.

"Who the fuck is that?"

"That's our girl, Foxy Brown and crew!" Victor said.

"Damn I'm glad their on our side!"

"No shit..!!"

Crystal and the girls kept firing until their shots had downed all five bodyguards, and a.k.a Kingpin Ruben was the only one standing. He had been shot several times but nothing fatal. Victor and Jordan rose up and saw only gun smoke in the air. Crystal walked out pissed!

"What's wrong baby, you got them!" Victor said.

"I'm pissed, because these muthafuckas shot-up my club, and killed Jake. I couldn't let them get away with that, I had to come out with my girls and set it off..! Is this that fat muthafucken Kingpin from Las Vegas that bitched about taking over our club?"

"Yeah babe that's him!" Jordan replied.

"Look at this place what the hell our we gonna do with him now?" Crystal asked.

Pow, pow,! "What the fuck did you do that for Jordan asked Victor?"

"Opps, we'll just say that he slipped and shot himself in the head! Twice..!"

"You're a fool..!" Crystal said as Jordan and Victor both kissed Crystal and she gave them both a passionate kiss on the lips.

"I'm not fucking with you two any more!" Crystal said.

"Who mentioned fucking? Did you mention fucking Jordan?"

'Naw man I didn't mention fucking, Victor!"

"Crystal did you mention fucking, because if you did, I have to warn you that I'm ready, how bout you Jordan...!"

"Yep! I'm ready too."

"How bout you Crystal?"

"Y'all better get some one in here to clean up this mess, and get rid of all these bodies that accidentally slipped and shot themselves."

"Aaah baby girl, don't trip! We both love you, so let's take it to the back room and have our self a Ménage A' Trois!" Victor slyly suggested.

"Man I don't want to see you naked!"

"Then keep your eyes close muthafucka!"

"Now you know that's wrong, and miss out on seeing Crystal's fine body!" Jordan said.

"Between the two of you, you'll never be able to keep up, so don't even try to go there, because this pussy don't play..!" Crystal said as she strutted her big ass across the floor to the back room and she unbuttoned her top to reveal her firm titties that stood at attention dropping her blouse to the floor, then she unzip her skin tight cat women's pants and then untied her six inch booths and kicked them to the side. Victor and Jordan's tongue was hanging out of their mouth, as their dicks stood erect at the thought of tonight's enjoyment.

The End

LOOK FOR *GHETTO THEORY PUBLISHING*
LATEST NEW RELEASES IN BOOK STORES AND
FOR PURCHASE ON

www.ghettotheory.com

www.Amazon.com
www.Smashword.com
www.Book Daily.com

*Now available in paperback on Amazon.com &
Ghetto Theory.com*

GHETTO THEORY PUBLISHING
Presents

Ghetto Games

Ghetto Games II, "the saga continues."

Am I My Sister's Keeper?

Natural Born gangster

**Rules of the Street Game that Every Hustler Should
Know...!**

Look for **"Ghetto Games III"**
Now Available 2014

Ghetto Games 1 ,
they are the hottest urban faction tales written and a
must read for anyone who enjoys the mind twisting
drama of the ghetto street life and passion that feed our
ambitions to struggle against all odds.

Ghetto Games II *"The Ghetto Saga Continues"*

This is the coldest and realest west coast gangster street classic that has ever been written. "If you like that west coast gangsta street shit... then you will love this!

GHETTO GAMES III

GHETTO THEORY
PUBLISHING PRESENT'S

G. PRINCE

The ghetto games continue in the
deadliest games ever played; a bloody game of revenge!

Revenge is the definition of Ghetto Games, as the three young rawest West Coast Kingpins, find themselves fighting a deadly battle against the worse enemies that they could ever want to face... Some scandalous, crooked ass cops from the L.A.P.D.

This is part three from the coldest West Coast gangsta tale ever told; Ghetto Games." A guaranteed page turner that is street certified and gangsta approved. The sequel continues!

DOUBLE TROUBLE

Smile Now.... Die Later

G. Prince
Ghetto Theory Publishing

This book is rated triple X for the extreme violent contents that has been realistically conveyed through the uncensorships that reflect the true urban struggles, and realities of the ghetto games.

GHETTO THEORY PUBLISHING

NATURAL BORN GANGSTER

"Don't judge me by my success if you don't know my struggles."

G. PRINCE

Money, sex, murder, betrayal, drugs, and revenge
only spells one thing, "Natural Born Gangster"